UNDE

THE HI

UNDERWORDS
THE HIDDEN CITY

THE

BOOKTRUST

LONDON SHORT STORY

COMPETITION ANTHOLOGY

Edited by Maggie Hamand

Published in 2005 by
The Maia Press Limited
82 Forest Road
London E8 3BH
www.maiapress.com

'Loose Change' by Andrea Levy first appeared in
The Independent on Sunday; 'Long Ago Yesterday' by
Hanif Kureishi first appeared in *The New Yorker* and
subsequently in *The Liberal* magazine; parts of 'P is for
Post-Black' by Diran Adebayo were broadcast on BBC
Radio 4 and appeared in *New Writing 12* (Picador)

ISBN 1 904559 14 X

A CIP catalogue record for this book is available from the
British Library

Printed and bound in Great Britain by Thanet Press

Published in collaboration with Booktrust
The publishers gratefully acknowledge support from
Arts Council England

CONTENTS

FOREWORD — *7*

Patrick Neate 'ALL WE LIKE SHEEP' — *11*

Shereen Pandit SHE SHALL NOT BE MOVED — *35*

Romesh Gunesekera THE LIBRARY — *47*

Max Mueller A CHAMPION — *57*

Andrea Levy LOOSE CHANGE — *67*

Alex Wheatle SHADE-ISM — *77*

Saeed Taji Farouky THE RAIN MISSED MY FACE
AND FELL STRAIGHT TO MY SHOES — *85*

Sarah Hall BEES — *101*

Paul T. Owen GUNFINGERS — *115*

Hanif Kureishi LONG AGO YESTERDAY — *135*

Louise Hocking SCRATCH THE SURFACE — *151*

Nicola Barker SALE — *161*

Fran Hill BEING 'MISS' — *175*

Diran Adebayo P IS FOR POST-BLACK — *185*

ABOUT THE AUTHORS — *197*

FOREWORD

This is the sixth anthology to result from the London Short Story Competition which was run this year by Booktrust, the national organisation bringing books and people together from the start. The theme of the competition was 'hidden' or 'secret' London and it aimed to find narrative pieces that would uncover aspects of this diverse city which are little known, whether in terms of activity, location or within the lives of its inhabitants.

Workshops were organised around the capital to encourage Londoners from all backgrounds to participate in the competition, which was promoted by leaflets and on the internet. The workshops were run by literature development agencies around London: one by Exiled Writers Ink, two by Collage Arts, two by Spread the Word, and three by West Words.

The Maia Press, a small independent publishing house of literary fiction which has made a commitment to the short story, was thrilled to be asked to publish this collection. As in past years, the winning entries were to be published together with eight stories by established writers who lived in London or whose stories were set there. Together with Yvonne Hook of

Booktrust, we set about approaching a variety of authors who would be prepared to contribute to this project. Many thanks to those who agreed to take part.

Around a hundred and fifty stories entered for the competition were reduced to a shortlist of eighteen by writer Shaun Levin, editor of the new literary magazine *Chroma*. The winning stories were chosen by myself as one of the Directors of The Maia Press, literary agent Laura Susijn, and James Smith, Literature Information Officer at Booktrust. We would also like to thank Kate Mervyn-Jones of Booktrust for her help during the book's production.

The overall winner of the competition was Shereen Pandit with her story, 'We shall not be moved'. A near runner-up was Max Mueller's 'A champion' closely followed by Saeed Taji Farouky's 'The rain missed my face and fell straight to my shoes'. The other three stories selected were also strong contenders. Many congratulations to all six authors for their excellent contributions to this vibrant, varied collection. They can hold their own with some of the biggest names in contemporary fiction.

Maggie Hamand
Director, The Maia Press

The short story is currently enjoying a renaissance, thanks partly to the Save Our Short Story campaign, originated by Arts Council England and now entering a new incarnation as The Story Board, a consortium of those who care about this very special form of fiction. The Story Board is coordinated by Booktrust and Scottish Booktrust. Funding from Arts Council England has been vital; advice and encouragement from the London literature team has been invaluable.

This collection shows that the short story is very much alive and well, in London as elsewhere, and has the power in a short space of time to shock, entertain and move us. These chronicles of the capital take us further and deeper than any Tube journey. Read this wonderful collection and enjoy.

Chris Meade
Director, Booktrust

Patrick Neate

'ALL WE LIKE SHEEP'

IT WAS MY IDEA that we should go. Of course Miriam thought it was hers since Mikey Armstrong was 'on her list'. I let her keep thinking that.

One evening, just before Miriam and I got hitched, we were watching *Friends*. It was a lovey-dovey night at a time when we still hadn't admitted that anything could go wrong. It was the episode where Ross and Rachel have the bright idea to select a fantasy list of five famous people each that they're allowed to shag without repercussions. It was my bright idea that Miriam and I should do likewise.

Since then, my list has remained unchanged; schoolboy pin-ups mostly. Let's be honest, if by some quirk of fate – last man on earth, Faustian pact, that kind of thing – I actually got the chance to cop off with any one of them, I wouldn't know where to begin. I've thought about it and it's true.

Recently, however (and when I say 'recently', I mean in the last couple of years), Miriam's chart has been repeatedly revamped; and with increasing enthusiasm and regularity too.

At various times, she has indulged most physical types (hunks, pretty boys, androgynes and so on) and numerous professions (including film stars [unsurprisingly] and celebrity chefs [more so]). On occasion, she has even ventured into extremities of appearance and occupation which, to me, could only be classified as fetishistic: three OAPs, two contemporary dictators and a grotesquely obese stand-up comedian, for example. Some of her selections may well have been illegal at various points in human history (if not the homosexuals or demigods then certainly the dead), some provoked pop psychological assumptions (celebrities that looked a little bit like her dad) and some verged on cruelty (celebrities that looked a little bit like me). None the less, as Miriam is so fond of saying, I'm not a very sensitive man so there was no particular name I took personally. Instead, it was the sheer volume and turnover of her choices which, when considered alongside the protracted dry spell in our sex life, eventually led me to conclude that her list-making might be symptomatic of problems in our marriage. Sometimes I figured that Miriam would rather edit aloud than talk about anything else. Mostly I admitted to myself that this suited me just fine.

At the time we went to see Mikey, I recall her chart was particularly diverse. I found it strange that its stars, though they'd never know it, would be forever associated in my head. I guess this is the nature of a list: it is the act of making it that truly connects the 'listees' rather than whether they actually have anything in common or not. Miriam's latest effort included the fat comic, a weatherman, a louche political pundit, a Machiavellian soap character (the character, mind, not the actor) and Mikey.

THE FOYER OF THE ALBERT HALL was packed breathless. There was a noticeable predominance of women and most of the men were noticeably appendages, only there under duress. One thing was clear: Mikey Armstrong appeared on many lists besides Miriam's.

Equally clearly, his appeal transcended boundaries of age, class and style. There were blowzy women of indeterminate mileage resplendent in unflattering block colour prints, mousey types renting binoculars for a better view, thin-lipped young professionals clutching briefcases and glasses of fizzy water, and surly students with piercings and ethnic tattoos garlanding their bare arms.

As I looked around it struck me that these women all had something in common beyond a passion for Mikey. They were all at least disappointed, perhaps even desperate. I could see it in every face. I could see it in every mannerism. I could see it in the way they clasped their tickets between blushing fingertips, the way they chattered to their friends or stood in taut silence with their partners.

If you're Miriam, of course, you might say something about how this observation is 'just typical' of my 'cynicism'. But you're not Miriam so you may as well trust my judgement. If you're on the ball, you might say something about how I've just contradicted my own theory of lists and, perhaps, that my observation tells you more about me than the women I was watching. Maybe. But you should trust that I know a disappointed, perhaps even desperate, woman when I see one.

The foyer had the urgent, slightly deranged atmosphere of a hen night.

I'D FIRST COME ACROSS Mikey Armstrong six months previously and there was something familiar about him from the start, even if I couldn't put my finger on exactly what. Miriam and I had sat down to our usual Saturday night in front of the goggle box and there he was, the musical guest on Parkinson.

To start with, Parky asked him a couple of straightforward questions and he answered them with easy, open charm. Yes, it was his first time on TV and he was kind of nervous. Yes, his album was out next week. His accent was transatlantic South London. Then Mikey sat down at the piano.

I couldn't tell you exactly what he played – some or other Chopin prelude, I think – although I remember his touch was exquisite. But I can tell you how he looked. He wore a pristine white shirt tucked into a pair of fitted jeans, his hair in tidy, shoulder-length dreadlocks, and a ring in his nose. And I can tell you how he moved, too: rhythmic convulsions punctuated by sudden jerks of his spine as if he'd been momentarily possessed by the music. And I can certainly tell you the effect he had on Miriam. As she watched transfixed, the fingernails of one hand raked my knee while the other slid between the buttons of my shirt.

I said, 'I bet he's a fag.'

She sat back and stared at me, irritated. 'Why do you always have to say that kind of thing?

'What kind of thing?'

She tutted but she still returned her hands to where they'd been roaming and now laid her head on my chest. I remember briefly thinking I might get lucky that night. I was wrong. That night my wife cried herself to sleep while I lay awake next to her, listening.

When Mikey finished playing, Parky led the applause. He said, 'Mikey Armstrong, ladies and gentlemen! Mikey Armstrong!'

There was cheering and some surprisingly raucous catcalls.

Mikey made further TV appearances: a daytime magazine, another chat show, a late-night music programme. He did several interviews in the broadsheet press. One proclaimed, 'The Saviour of Classical Music'. Another detailed his biography: London to his early teens and then the States on various scholarships and the like. Another ran beneath a single word headline: 'Star!' So it was official.

With hindsight it's bizarre that it took me so long to put two and two together. But you need to understand that Mikey

Armstrong had a charisma that held no echoes of the kid I'd known. Besides, he was now slim and tall with dreadlocks and a nose ring. Besides, it had been pushing twenty years and I'd known him when his parents were together and he was still called Michael Brannon.

MIRIAM IS NOT the kind of woman who cries. I've always liked that about her. In the decade I've known her, I've only seen her cry twice; the second time was the night Mikey Armstrong appeared on *Parkinson*, the first was the last time we ate chicken kievs.

I'd got home before her so I was cooking. I had Chelsea v Fulham on the radio. Miriam came in about eight. She asked what we were eating. I turned the radio off. I told her we were having chicken kievs with mashed potato and salad. She hovered in the kitchen a while. She asked how my day was. I said it was OK. I asked about her day. She said it was OK too.

She went to the fridge and emptied the dregs of a bottle of white into a tumbler. She wandered into the living room. I heard a burst of laughter from the TV. I put the football on again. A couple of minutes later Miriam reappeared to shut the kitchen door.

We ate supper on our laps, side by side on the sofa, like we always did. I can't remember what was on the telly. I can't remember whether Miriam was already in a mood.

When Miriam speared the chicken with her knife, a jet of hot butter squirted out and over her blouse. She swore. I think I might have chuckled. I think I might even have said something like, 'That's kievs for you.'

Certainly she said, 'It's not funny.'

'Calm down. It's only a bit of butter. It'll come out in the wash.'

That was when she started crying.

I asked her what was wrong. She shook her head. It took her a moment to answer. She lifted her kiev on her fork and said, 'Is this it?'

I didn't know what to say to that so I said: 'It's all there was in the freezer,' although I knew that wasn't what she was getting at.

I put my plate on the coffee table. I'd gone off my food. I rested my hand on Miriam's arm for a moment. Then I took it back and sat with my elbows on my knees staring at the grain of the floorboards between my feet. I stayed like that for a while, Miriam snivelling quietly next to me, before she eventually started talking.

She said she hadn't expected our life together to be like this. She said that we had nothing in common apart from the fact that we were married and that we lived in the same flat. If I were totally honest, I'd have told her this was enough to be going on with but I held my tongue. She said that she couldn't go on. She said that we never did anything as a couple any more, not like before. If I were totally honest, I'd have pointed out that we'd never done anything as a couple beyond go to the same mid-table London university where we'd hung out with the same group of mates. But I held my tongue again. She stared at me. She said, why did we get married anyway? If I were totally honest, I'd have told her that we got married because, for better or worse, that's what people like us did. But I'm not totally honest. In fact I'm not honest at all.

Instead I said, 'So what do you want to do?'

She looked at me and sighed and smiled weakly. It was a smile so weak that its disdain quite took me by surprise. 'What do I want to do?' she said. 'Why don't you talk to me? You're always so pragmatic.' She meant it as an insult.

I said, 'I am. I am pragmatic. Look . . . Look . . .'

ALTHOUGH IT WAS MY IDEA that we should go and see
Mikey Armstrong, it was Miriam who booked the tickets and
I confess that, when we took our seats right in front of the
boxes, spitting distance from the stage, I spent at least a couple
of minutes calculating how much they must have cost. It was
at least a couple of minutes, therefore, before I even took in
Mikey's set-up, let alone the attitude of my wife.

The stage was bare apart from the piano at the front and
half a dozen podiums at differing heights dotted around. All of
these podiums were empty apart from the highest one,
upstage, that held a set of turntables. Behind the turntables,
there was a DJ – a kid who looked about sixteen – deftly
mixing rap records before the appearance of the main attraction. I had no doubts about this DJ's skill but, to judge from
the bemused looks of the people around us, it wasn't just me
who wondered what this had to do with classical music.

Behind the DJ hung an enormous screen on which were
projected various clips of footage and still photographs. Sometimes the screen showed a sequence of a celebrated conductor
at work, and his frantic movements were somehow synched to
the DJ's tricks. It was really quite clever. Sometimes the screen
showed a black-and-white photograph of Mikey. It was the
famous picture that everyone knew. In it, Mikey was climacti-
cally rigid, his head thrown back, his face somehow ecstatic,
his dreadlocks flailing, several drops of sweat caught in the
lights to make some kind of halo. The composition of this
picture was copied from an even more famous picture of Bob
Marley. The only difference was that Mikey was white and a
classically trained pianist.

It struck me that it isn't enough to be good any more, you
also have to be cool. It wasn't the first time I'd thought this
and it wasn't intended as a judgement. It was just a statement
of fact.

Miriam was holding my hand. I only noticed this when she began to squeeze my fingers as the lights dimmed and a ripple of applause built into unrestrained cheering and some undignified screams. My wife now holds my hand as if it were a baby's comfort blanket or an executive's stress reliever. It is not an action that signifies connection with me, rather that her attention is fully focused elsewhere.

I didn't see Mikey come on stage because I was looking at Miriam. She was bolt upright and craning her neck for a better view. Her eyes were wide, her mouth slightly open and her lips pouting, as if she were blowing a smoke ring. I recognised the expression. When we first got together, Miriam liked us to have sex in front of the mirror so that she could watch herself. She got on all fours and I knelt behind her and pulled her head back by the hair. After a while, this became the only sexual position in which Miriam would come; and this was her orgasm face. I watched fascinated.

She was wearing a halter-neck top and she'd recently cropped her hair boyishly short. I could see the tendons of her neck strung out like rigging, and the skin of her shoulders looked transparent over lean but well-defined musculature. She suddenly looked very beautiful and very old, and a little bit like a very convincing transvestite. She also looked totally unfamiliar. It's funny how in one instant you can realise that it's possible to know someone both intimately and not at all.

ON THE NIGHT we ate chicken kievs for the last time and I saw Miriam cry for the first, I made a proposition.

'Look . . .' I said. 'Look . . . so what if we don't do anything together any more. That's easy enough to change, right? Let's just each choose one activity that we can both participate in.'

Miriam was still sniffing but I could tell I'd piqued her interest. She said, 'Like what?'

'Like whatever. That's the point.'

It took Miriam less than thirty seconds to name her activity and I got the feeling she only took that long because she was choosing from a broad list of options. She said she wanted us to join a gym and she must have noticed my face fall because she said, 'I just want to be healthy. I don't want us to spend the rest of our lives as couch potatoes. Besides, I'm getting fat.'

'Don't be silly.'

'Well. *You're* definitely getting fat. Come on. I want us to join a gym.'

'OK.'

'Really?'

'OK. We'll join a gym.'

She smiled then. She said she thought it might be fun. I kept my thoughts to myself. Then she asked, 'What about you? What do you want to do together?'

I didn't know what to say. I hadn't figured that far ahead and I didn't really want to 'do' anything together because I was happy enough with the way things were, wasn't I? But I couldn't say that. I considered suggesting that we went to the movies once a week. But I knew that wouldn't wash either. I tried to think of something I used to do in the past that I didn't do any more and that I missed. For a while I couldn't come up with a single thing. Then I had an idea that was so right I couldn't believe it hadn't occurred to me before. It was so right that it made feel a little seasick to think about it. I said, 'I want us to join a choir.'

'A choir?' Miriam looked at me like I'd gone mad.

'Yeah.'

'A *choir*?' She made the word sound distasteful, as if I'd

suggested sharing a crack pipe or a night's dogging in a lay-by. 'You can't sing.'

'Yeah, I can. It's just you've never heard me. I can sing. In fact, at school I was a choral scholar.'

'What?' Miriam laughed uneasily. 'I never knew that.'

'Quite,' I said. I don't know what I meant by that. Or rather I know what I meant by it but I don't know what it was supposed to achieve.

We both did some research. A couple of weeks later we were inducted into a gym on the Fulham Palace Road. Miriam was told she was of median weight and fitness for her age and build. Apparently I was the fat and breathless side of average. A couple of weeks after that we joined a gospel choir.

It wasn't a real gospel choir, just a beginners' class in an Acton parish hall. There were thirty of us. We would rehearse twice a week for three months, building towards a concert in the church. I loved it.

The choir master-cum-teacher was an over-enthusiastic, 24-year-old black guy called Errol who was either an advert for religious faith or a warning against it, depending on your point of view. Mine varied. The pianist was an earnest and elderly black woman called Joy who played that piano as if she wanted to cause it pain.

'You've got to believe, people! You've got to believe what you're singing!' Errol shouted, beaming. And I did. But the others struggled to be heard over Joy's vindictive chords.

I mention Errol's and Joy's race and ages only because they were the only black people involved in this gospel choir and the only ones outside the thirty-something age bracket. Apart from Miriam and me, there were fifteen single women who really just wanted a decent, kind, sympathetic man and surely that wasn't too much to ask; and thirteen single men who weren't it. And then there was Miriam. And me. I'm simplifying, naturally.

We went to five rehearsals. On the way home after the fifth, Miriam told me that I sang too loudly. Too loudly for what?

I sang too loudly for the rest of the choir, she said, and besides I didn't have a gospel voice anyway and, to be honest, it was embarrassing.

We had a fight. I told her the last thing I wanted to do was embarrass her, perish the thought. I told her we wouldn't go back. She said I was being childish. She could talk. I told her that it was no good because now I was embarrassed too. We didn't go back.

Errol left three messages. He said that he was really disappointed and didn't we see we were letting everyone down? Miriam and I made up over unspoken guilt and the spoken opinion that Errol was a smug pain in the arse and, in fact, that was the trouble with born-agains.

I stopped going to the gym about a month later. Miriam thought this was retaliation. It wasn't. I explained to her that I just hated the changing room: the macho atmosphere, all those men comparing their biceps and pecs, it wasn't my kind of thing. She laughed at me.

'That place is a roid factory,' I told her. 'It's all meatheads and queens. Why couldn't we go to a normal gym?'

She said I was being childish again.

Miriam still works out four, five, sometimes even six times a week. It's another wedge between us.

FROM THE MOMENT Mikey Armstrong announced his first set, Miriam was spellbound. Then again, I suspect he could have come out and played the spoons for an hour and my wife would have claimed it the most inspiring show she'd ever seen.

As for me, overall I thought it was decidedly average; a triumph only of style over content. To judge from the audience reaction, however, I'll admit I was in a minority of one.

Mikey certainly played well enough and he still had undeniable presence. He opened, for example, with a movement from Liszt's First Piano Concerto and, though his interpretation was a little polished for my tastes, any flaws were more than compensated for in the extraordinary physicality of his playing. Alone on stage and picked out by a single spot, his performance was also projected on to the giant screen behind so that you couldn't miss a single twist in his expression, whip of his neck or thrash of his dreads. If this sounds too awful to you then that's only because of the inadequacies of my description. I mean, the idea of it *was* indisputably awful – crass and over the top – but the reality was simply hypnotising to watch; even for me. I don't think Mikey was acting. He wasn't *re*acting to the music either. It was more like he was playing the music and the music was playing him at the same time; like he was the personification of every phrase. I can't explain it better.

In my opinion it went downhill from there. In fact, the show reminded me of one of those 'An audience with . . .' TV programmes, when some celebrity wheels out their famous friends for duets, jokes or repartee; because, for the next ninety minutes, Mikey hardly performed alone again. Instead, when he introduced each piece, he was joined on stage by some or other guest who took their place on one or other podium.

Some of these collaborations were more successful than others: he played Vivaldi with a premier Russian violinist, Mozart's songs accompanying a second-tier Spanish tenor, snatches of Beethoven bizarrely interspersed with input from DJ Tick. But the nadir was reached when one of Mikey's own compositions was used to underscore ten minutes of spoken word performed by a super-fashionable New York novelist, best-known as one of the McSweeney's crowd. For me, the whole thing stank of cabaret but the packed house lapped it up.

Then Mikey introduced what he said would be his last piece of the night. It was another of his compositions and he'd perform it alone. He told us it was a very personal work and admitted he was still toying with its structure. He told us it was the first time he'd felt comfortable enough to air it in public. The Albert Hall cheered. He told us it was called 'Julian Number 1' and, when he said that, he paused for a second and smiled a little as if there may have been something he was neglecting to mention. He said he hoped we enjoyed it.

How can I describe this piece of music? I might tell you that it was based on a simple chord sequence that rose and fell; by turns lingering and abrupt, drawing and breaking; a single melodic theme occasionally tiptoeing over the top. I might tell you that the screen behind the stage remained blank throughout. I don't know whether this was the point or Mikey had only decided to include this new work at the very last minute. I might tell you that, as he played, Mikey was, for once, almost motionless. But I think that to try to describe the music or performance is probably pointless, certainly beyond me.

It is, therefore, only the audience reaction that I can relay with any confidence: they were sympathetic but nonplussed. They were now, I realised, so used to a spectacle that they equated *that* with good music and couldn't hear beauty in such a raw and honest form. But I could and I was quite profoundly moved.

I am not asserting some kind of special quality in myself. As I've already told you, I'm not a sensitive man. Perhaps it was just the personal connections that started a chain reaction that had my palms sweating and my heart beating a little faster. 'Julian Number 1' made me think of Julian Furze; a name I'd long blanked from my memory. From there, of course, it was a small step to Michael Brannon and I found myself staring at the superstar pianist with a growing sense of certainty. Then, when the gentle melodic line indisputably echoed Handel, I was sure.

Apart from my clammy hands that were clasped in my lap, I don't know what physical manifestation there was of my undeniably emotional state but there must have been one because Miriam touched me on the shoulder.

'What's the matter with you?' she whispered. She was looking at me like and as a stranger.

'Nothing,' I said.

MICHAEL BRANNON AND I started at the same London private school in the same term. We had nothing in common except that we were both music scholars and both thirteen years old. I'd arrived from a small suburban prep to be lead treble in the school choir. Back then, I was tiny for my age, very self-conscious about it and desperate for acceptance. I wore all the right clothes, cut my hair in the latest fashion and would do and say almost anything to fit in. But being a choirboy wasn't exactly a password to popularity. Michael, on the other hand, was from a state school and a prodigy on the piano. You wouldn't have known it to look at him. He wore thick glasses and he had these tight curls that sprouted from his head like springs. He was big – not fat nor tall but burly and clumsy – something that made his grace on any form of keyboard all the more extraordinary. He also seemed completely unfazed by the fact that our peers took the piss out of us all the time. I remember he was a quiet kid but I also remember him saying on more than one occasion, 'I only came here for the music.' He didn't even seem to care when briefly, for a day or two at the end of the spring term, we were both known as 'gay boys'.

That started after the run-through for the Easter concert. The concert itself was to take place on the last Sunday in the chapel when the audience would be parents, governors, alumni and the like. But on the preceding Wednesday there was a full rehearsal which was compulsory attendance for the whole school. Among other things, our choir teamed up with the girls' choir from the convent school down the road to perform excerpts from *The Messiah* accompanied by Michael on the organ. It was me, however, who sang the soprano aria 'I Know That My Redeemer Liveth'.

The next day I was changing for football (also compulsory) and down to my underpants when a group of sixth-formers appeared in the junior locker room. They were headed by the eighteen-year-old son of a supermarket millionaire who wore this flat, sneering expression permanently embedded in his face like roadkill in tarmac. His name was Julian Furze. He was the coolest kid in the school and known to everybody as 'Number 1'.

When he saw me, he said, 'Who's this pretty girl?'

I laughed. I may as well be honest: I was flattered by this attention.

'I saw the concert. Fuck! You sing high!' Briefly, he warbled at me in his falsetto. His cronies were laughing too. Then he said, 'Have you even got a single fucking pube?'

'Loads,' I said.

'Show me.'

'No.'

He shrugged. He said, 'Show me. You don't have to show me your girly little dick. Just show me your pubes.'

The older boys had now surrounded me. I said, 'No.' I was short of breath.

The next thing I knew I'd been lifted on to the wooden bench in the middle of the locker room, flat on my back. There were several pairs of hands pulling at my pants but I clung on to them. Then the elastic ripped and I was naked. I tried to cover myself but they pinned my hands. Of course I didn't have any pubic hair and what's more my small, 13-year-old penis was stiff, poking out from my groin at a right angle like an insulting middle finger. I can't explain why. I think it was the excitement, the fear. I was still giggling even as I cried.

Number 1 howled with delight at the sight of me. 'Fuck me!' he said. 'The gay boy loves it! Turn him over!' And they did. They flipped me and pushed me down so that my groin was squashed painfully against the wood and my buttocks exposed. He said, 'Hold him down!' And they did.

Looking back on it now, I don't think they were actually going to rape me (even though I was convinced of it at the time). I mean, for all the horrors of that place, it wasn't even a boarding school, let alone a prison, and I know most of those sixth-formers were having more-or-less successful sex with their more-or-less willing girlfriends from the convent. I mean, what I'm saying is that there was no culture of sexual violence and I don't reckon this mob were any more repressed than your average teenager, and they would probably have been happy with my abject humiliation. But I could be wrong and I'll never know because at that moment Michael appeared, whirling a football boot around his head and screaming obscenities at the top of his voice.

All the bullies froze for a second. It's funny, but in retrospect I think they were shocked by his language more than anything. This was a London private school, you see, and it valued cynicism and sarcastic put-downs. But Michael was using brutal words that I assume he'd learned at his previous educational institution. I guess it was all a bit too much for these well-brought-up bastards.

In the instant that the sixth-formers stepped back, Michael made a beeline for Number 1 and hit him hard over the back of the head and then again. I took the opportunity to gather the scraps of my underwear and run for it. I made it out of the junior locker room and into the main changing area where I was immediately halted by a shout from the sports master: 'Stop! Boy!'

Behind me, I could hear the bullies and my lone defender scattering.

The gossip spread like wildfire around the school; not that Michael had hit Number 1, of course, but that I was gay and Michael was my boyfriend.

AS THE LAST CHORD of 'Julian Number 1' hummed into the gods at the Albert Hall, the audience didn't seem to know how to respond. There was polite applause and a few people shouted 'More!' but you could almost hear their silent caveat, ' – but we're talking about more of what went before. Not *that*.'

Mikey Armstrong stood up and bowed with a flourish. His face was once again projected behind him and, to me, he looked suddenly and deeply saddened; although whether this was because of the music he'd just played or the music he was about to play, I don't know. Maybe, in fact, his sadness was a projection of my own.

Without waiting for further requests, Mikey sat down again and launched into his encore. It was a classical interpolation of 'Bohemian Rhapsody' by Queen and one by one

Mikey's guests rejoined him on stage. The DJ cut in snatches of the original recording, the violinist added a variation of the string section, the novelist added a couple of stanzas of poetry based on the line 'I'm just a poor boy from a poor family' and the tenor sang 'Thunderballs and lightning / Very very frightening / Me!' at the top of his register.

The climax came, however, with the notorious guitar solo. A silhouette was highlighted on the big screen and then, suddenly, there was Brian May himself, his guitar shrieking in his hands. The Albert Hall went bonkers.

If this sounds too awful to you, then, again, that's only because of the inadequacies of my description. However awful I've made it sound, I swear it was more awful still. None the less, what distressed me most was not the music, but the fact it was Mikey playing it.

I would be lying if I told you I'd thought a lot about Michael Brannon in the preceding twenty years but, in that instant, he became a counterpoint to every significant decision I'd made since the age of thirteen.

I know that all my choices – from giving up singing as soon as my voice broke, to marrying Miriam – have been taken with a willingness to compromise, a resignation to an easy life, a desire to fit in. I don't have a particularly high opinion of myself and I'm able to accept this as fact. However, it's a fact that is only made bearable by a belief that there are other people of principle who are singular of purpose and prepared to be different. Suddenly I realised that Mikey was at the top of this list and I felt desperately let down. I felt let down because this was the boy who'd repeatedly said, 'I only came here for the music,' and yet here he was compromising that very thing. Of course I recognised that his compromises were of a different order to mine but that didn't matter because, as far as I was concerned, he was of a different order to me too. And as the audience rose at the beginning of an extended standing ovation, I stayed in my seat and all I could think was, 'He was supposed to be better.'

THE DAY AFTER the incident in the locker room, Julian Furze found me in the library at lunchtime. His mates sat on my left and right and behind me so I couldn't escape and he flopped down on the other side of the desk. Number 1 had a swelling stud mark above his right eye and it didn't take me long to figure out that Michael had embarrassed him and, as the coolest kid in the school, he had to be seen to do something.

He said, 'You still got a hard-on, gay boy?' and, while the guys on either side of me held my shoulders, the one behind reached into my trousers and began to painfully hoist up my boxers.

The only librarian on duty was a fifth-former so there was no point making a fuss. Instead I just hissed, 'Please leave me alone.'

'Fine,' he said. 'Just tell me where your boyfriend is.'

I led them to the rehearsal room in the music school without complaint. I didn't see it as betrayal, simply pragmatism. As we walked, some of Number 1's mates joked with me. They slapped me on the backside and I said, 'Get off!' And they said, 'You love it!' It was a kind of popularity.

When we went into the rehearsal room Michael didn't look up. He was practising the 'All We Like Sheep' chorus at top speed, playing the same sixteen-bar section over and over again, faster and faster, perfecting his fingering. Even when Number 1 said 'I want a word with you, gay boy!' Michael didn't look up.

'Not now,' he muttered. 'I'm working.'

'I said I want a word with you.'

'I said I'm working.'

Number 1 stood right next to Michael and cuffed him around the head.

Michael said, 'I only came here for the music.' But there was no plea in his voice and his hands didn't skip a note.

Now, Number 1 leant on the piano and cuffed him again, harder this time. Finally Michael had to look up, though his fingers still leapt flawlessly around the keys. He stared at the older boy unblinking. He spoke quietly. 'Fuck off you posh cunt,' he said.

Numbers 1's mates gasped and snorted, half-laughter and half-disbelief. Number 1 looked totally thrown. He said, 'You . . . you . . . I'll fucking . . .' But while he was an expert with cynicism and sarcasm, the coolest kid in the school was a beginner when it came to coarse. One of the others started to giggle and Number 1 looked at him wildly. Like I said, he had to be seen to do something so, in a moment of macho madness, he took hold of the hinged piano cover and brought it slamming down.

He broke Michael's right wrist and two knuckles on his left hand. I was called into the headmaster's office to testify. I kept it simple. Number 1 was expelled. It was, of course, the term before his A-Levels and it caused quite a scandal. The fact that I was a witness to the whole thing did wonders for my profile. Michael was taken off to the hospital and never came back to the school, and the next time I saw him was on *Parkinson*. The music teacher had to play all Michael's parts at the Christmas concert. Everybody said I sang beautifully but I'd already made up my mind and, when my voice started to break the following spring, it was an escape route.

WE WERE STILL FILING out of the Albert Hall when Miriam began her tirade. She said she couldn't believe I hadn't joined in the standing ovation. Why had I bothered coming if I was so determined not to enjoy myself? She said it was typical. She said I didn't have a sensitive bone in my body.

For once, I reacted. I said, 'You don't know what you're fucking talking about.'

Momentarily she was surprised into silence. Then she told me she was going to try and get Mikey Armstrong's autograph and I'd better not have a problem with that. There was more silence but this time it was filled with something like loathing.

Outside the stage door I felt ridiculous. There was a gaggle of forty-odd women hanging around. And me.

After ten minutes, I said to Miriam, 'Let's go.' But she just gave me a look.

Then Brian May appeared and some people shrieked and the majority of the crowd dispersed, following him to his limo. I realised that Mikey's fame was, as all fame is, relative. There were probably half a dozen of us die-hards left.

When Mikey finally came out, the women, including Miriam, rushed forward and pressed their programmes on him. I hung around at the back and watched. He signed all the programmes without complaint and even posed for a photograph or two but there was something missing in his expression. Whereas six months earlier on *Parkinson* he'd been indisputably himself, he now had a public face. He could smile or frown or even laugh but it was all automatic, superficial and therefore at some level, I suppose, disrespectful (or was that only if anybody noticed?). I could have been looking in a mirror.

Then Mikey saw me and he flickered recognition. He brushed past the last proffered programme (my wife's, as it turned out) and came over. He said something and smiled a genuine smile. I replied and smiled genuinely too. Then he turned and headed off to a limo of his own. As I watched him go, I found Miriam standing next to me. She was staring at me, curious and a little bit awe-struck, as if I'd been touched by greatness. 'Do you know him?' she asked.

'Not really.'

'What did he say to you?'

'He said, "All we like sheep".'

She blinked. 'What did you say?'

'I said, "Have gone astray".'

'What does that mean?'

'From *The Messiah*.'

She tutted at me but she wasn't really impatient. She said, 'I know it's from *The Messiah* but what does it mean?'

I looked at her. 'It means I want to tell you something.'

I wanted to tell her about a time when Mikey Armstrong and I were on the same list pinned to a noticeboard beneath the heading 'Music Scholars 1986/7'. I wanted to tell her the story I've just told you. In fact, I wanted to tell her lots of things and ask her lots of things too. I wanted to tell her about her husband and ask her about my wife. I thought we could take it from there.

Shereen Pandit

SHE SHALL NOT BE MOVED

I SWEAR, IF IT HADN'T BEEN SO LATE, I'd have done something about it. Or if the previous two number 201 buses hadn't vanished into thin air. Or if it hadn't been so cold. Or if I didn't have Mariam with me, almost turning blue with the cold. Yes, I would definitely have done something about it, there and then. I would have given him a piece of my mind. And them.

But the thing is, it *was* late, and the buses *hadn't* come for more than an hour. And this being London, it *was* pretty darned cold *and* there was Mariam, shivering next to me. So I was highly pleased, I tell you, when that bus finally pulled up. I paid. That's another thing, it was the last change I had on me and I couldn't afford to get chucked off, could I?

Anyhow, this bus finally comes, I put Mariam up alongside me, while I pay. Then I try to move her along into the bus ahead of me. Only we can't move. The aisle's blocked by this huge woman, with a pram in the middle of the aisle. She seems to be Somali, from her clothes – long dark dress, hair covered with a veil, like nuns used to wear, arms covered to the wrists, nothing but face and hands showing. The driver shouts at me to move down the bus, only I can't because of the pram. I'm about to say to him, 'Well, get this woman to move out of the way' – it's one of those modern buses with a special place for prams – when I see what the problem is.

There are these two women, sitting in those fold-up seats in the pram space. White, fiftyish, wrinkles full of powder and grey roots under the blonde rinse, mouths like dried-up prunes, both of them. One of them's wearing a buttoned-up cardie like Pauline in *East Enders*. The other one's wearing a colourless crumpled and none-too-clean mac of some kind. The big-breasted, big-bottomed type. Both looked strong enough in the arm to lift a good few down the pub every night.

They're sitting right under that notice which says: 'Please allow wheelchair users and those with prams priority in using this space.' Which means these two are supposed to get up so the Somali woman can put her pram in the space left when their seats fold up. Only they're staring hard out of the window, pretending they haven't heard a word of what's going on, and if they did, it's nothing to do with them.

As I said, they didn't look like the kind to tackle unless you wanted a real scene. I wouldn't have put it past the likes of them to use some pretty rough language, regardless of whether there were kids around. Me, I don't like exposing Mariam to unpleasantness. So I turn to the driver, who's still yelling down the aisle from behind his glassed-in box. I reckon it's his job to tell the women to move. I mean, why should I do his dirty work?

There are two empty seats right opposite the women. They can just move over the aisle. I look hard at them, trying to will them to look around. They finally can't resist looking round to see the havoc they've caused. They're still trying to be nonchalant, but you can see this gleam of satisfaction in their eyes, their mouths growing even thinner as they jam their lips grimly together, as if to say: 'That'll show you who's boss!'

I take the chance to point the empty seats out to them. Politely. I'm doing as my Mum said when I was young, always show them we're better. So, even though I've got a small kid with me, I'm not scrambling to grab the seat. Usually I let Mariam sit down because buses jerking around can be dangerous for kids, especially kids like Mariam, small for her age and skinny to boot. But do these old so-and-sos take the seats I'm pointing out to them? Not likely. They look at me, then look at the seats as if they're a pile of dog dirt I'm offering. Then they mutter something to each other, turn up their noses and stare out the window again, like it's nothing to do with them.

The Somali woman, meantime, has squashed herself tight up against the side of the aisle, just below the stairs. If anyone really wants to, they can squeeze past and go on upstairs. Her face is tight too. Lips set. Eyes blank. Head held high. She looks like a haughty queen. She's done her best to accommodate other passengers by leaving them what inches she can, and now she just shuts off and looks into space.

Through all this, the driver's been yelling on and off. Finally, his door swings open – the glassed-in bit leading into the bus, I mean. Right, I think, here he comes, he's going to make the old witches move. He's not scared of them, big strapping bloke, he doesn't have to be scared of anyone or anything. Besides, he's got right on his side. They can't even complain among themselves, let alone to his employers, that he's taking sides with the Somali women just because they're both black.

But oh no! He comes at this Somali woman and yells at her that either she folds up the pram or she leaves the bus. He's all over her, leaning right into her face and shouting. I reckon he's going to hit her. I hate violence and I turn Mariam's face away. I don't like her seeing ugliness like this. The Somali woman doesn't give an inch. Except to turn aside disdainfully because this bloke's spit is flying in her face. Pulling her wrapper more

closely about her, she says scornfully that she's not doing
either. And you can see why not. Her baby's asleep in the pram
and she's already got another small one hanging on to her. One
hand on the pram, another on the toddler.

Her face is full of contempt for this driver, but her voice
isn't rude or loud or anything. Just firm. She's paid, she's got
these kids, she's staying put. He shouts and storms. Eventually
he gives up and goes back and starts the bus so it jerks and she
and the kid and the pram nearly go flying, except for the pram
being stuck. Me, I'm totally shocked at his attitude. I'm really
building up a head of steam here. If it wasn't for all the stuff I
said before, at this stage I really would have given him a go.
But he's gone back and there's nothing I can do about him.

I tell the Somali woman to sit down in the empty seat,
thinking she can at least hold the small one on her lap and
maybe I could steady the pram while Mariam sits next to her.
She shakes her head wordlessly. It's like she's used up all her
words on the driver. I reckon maybe, in spite of her looking so
proud and firm, she's too timid to give the women a go. Maybe
she's worried, being black and a foreigner, probably a refugee
and all. Maybe she also doesn't like a scene and is already
embarrassed enough by the women. Maybe if she'd said something to them directly, I would have backed her. But how could
I go and attack them out of the blue, make them move, if she's
not saying anything to them?

The two women, deciding that they aren't having enough
fun, start a loud conversation with each other about how
they're not getting up, no way. Cardie reckons to Mac that
'they' – meaning women with prams, or does she mean black
women? – just pretend 'they' want to park the pram and then
snatch the seats. 'They' want everything their way. Definitely
black people this time. And on and on they go. I'm fuming,

among other things, because Mariam is being subjected to all this racist hogwash. But what's the point in having a go? It'll only lead to a row lasting the whole bus ride and I probably will get chucked off then for stirring. Even if I'm in the right. They can say what they like about anti-racist laws, but I've yet to see them stop people like these two slinging their poison around.

I look at the other passengers in the second half of the bus, past the stairs. All white. No one's saying anything, no one's seeing anything, no one's hearing anything. Not their business. Mariam starts to nudge me and whispers to me to tell the driver to tell the old witches to move. She doesn't call them that, though. Calls them 'those two ladies'. Ladies my back-side.

Mariam's language is polite, but this is a kid with attitude. Got it from me, I guess. I used to be known as a kid with atti-tude, too. 'They can have our seats,' she says loudly. I nod, but say nothing. Mariam decides to go on, so I feel like really nudging her hard, only I don't hold with hurting kids. They are the problem, she says even more loudly. I look at them again, still saying nothing. I'm still thinking that with the Somali woman saying nothing to them and the driver on their side, I'm going to end up outside in the cold with Mariam, minus the fare, if I take them on.

This is what I'm thinking, but not saying to Mariam. Kids, there are things they just don't understand. I mean, Mariam would definitely not get to her dance lesson on time and then she'd be right miffed. And then there's the bus fare and the fees and the time and everything all wasted.

Mariam glares at the women. She glares at me. I know what she's thinking. How many times have I told her to stand up against wrongdoing. How many times have I pushed her into standing up against bullies at school, whether they're bullying her or someone else. And her only such a small kid for her age.

We try to bring her up thinking about right and wrong. Like how many times have I told her that I'm only living in this miserable country because I'd got into trouble back home, fighting for our rights. There are political posters and slogans all over the house. One of them's got Pastor Neumuller's speech: 'First they came for the Jews . . .' and all that. She knows, all right. She knows that I should be speaking up for this Somali woman.

And here I'm saying nothing, doing nothing. Every once in a while, when people get on and mutter about the aisle being blocked, the driver shouts at the Somali woman. She stands there like a rock. Cardie and Mac have restarted their loud conversation about 'them' wanting to take everything over. I laugh in their faces and start agreeing loudly with Mariam, but I don't say anything to them. The bus is filling up. At a couple of stops some pretty yobbo-looking types get on. You know, tattoos, earrings all over their faces, hair sticking up. The type that I can't afford to get tangled with. I don't fancy a boot in my face, or in Mariam's, while those two probably watch and cheer. The yobbos just squeeze past the Somali woman. It's a couple of blokes in collars and ties who swear at her before they force a path upstairs, nearly making her let go of the pram and fall. You can't always tell by appearances, can you?

Then the bus empties a bit. Another middle-aged woman gets on, about the same age as the two trouble-makers. But this one's sort of frailer-looking. Now my Mum, when we were kids, she'd only have given us what for if we didn't get up and offer our seats to older people. I've still got the habit drilled into me. I don't like Mariam getting up, like I said, in case she falls, so usually I give up my seat. But this time, I sit tight. Mariam gives me a questioning look, then makes to get up for this new old lady, but I pull her down. Call me a reverse racist if you like, but if those white women won't get up for the Somali woman, then I'm not giving my seat or my kid's to one of their kind. No way. I didn't start this.

Now they start a loud conversation about 'their' manners. Meaning me. I glare at them and say nothing. I can feel Mariam wriggling with impatience for me to mouth off at them. But I reckon with the driver on their side, even against this poor woman with her pram and her kids, what chance have I got? He'd probably call the police for me, if I gave them lip. And guess whose side the police would be on! So I glare and sit tight. I stare straight ahead, like this old lady standing is nothing to do with me. I can feel my lips tighten with satisfaction at getting back at the other two. See how they feel when it's one of their kind getting a dose of it.

But I'm feeling right small inside. I feel like a real sod. Not only for not standing up for the Somali woman, but for not giving my seat to the old white woman. Plus Mariam starts hassling about getting up for the old woman. I almost blow my top at Mariam. I mean, can't she see what I'm doing? Standing up to them? I pull her down again and glare at her, whispering, 'No!' fiercely at her as she struggles to stand up and give her seat to the old woman standing.

Then I feel like a right idiot, getting upset at Mariam. The kid's only doing what she's been taught. I make my excuses to Mariam, but she's not taking any notice of me. She doesn't exactly look like she wants to cry, like when she's mad at me, though. Her face is just the same as usual, not swelling up and going red like it always does before she starts to cry, but her eyes have that sad, lost, grief-stricken look. I sit there feeling right helpless. I'm trying to remember where I know that look from.

The bus is coming to a main shopping area, people are walking around with holly-printed plastic bags full of goodies. That makes me remember when Mariam had that look on her face. She had it when she woke up in the night last Christmas and found her Dad stuffing her stocking. I feel sick at the thought of what she's thinking of me. The thing is, what can I do? You can teach kids to stand up against bullies, but sometimes they've got to learn that discretion is the better part of valour. I start to explain, but Mariam isn't taking any notice. She looks again at the old woman swaying about on the bus, trying to hold on to prevent herself falling. Then she gives me a look – like I've chucked away her favourite teddy bear.

At last we get to Wood Green and the trouble-makers get off, slinging a last few barbs over their shoulders. At that, the Somali woman finally snaps. She lets go of the pram and leans out the doorway and shouts 'Racists!' after them. They're still hurling abuse at her, as if they were the injured parties, as they disappear into the crowd, everybody staring. But, thank God, it's Wood Green and the sea of faces staring interestedly at us is as much black as white.

The Somali woman starts to struggle to turn the pram so she can get off too. I offer to help her, muttering to her that she should report the driver. What's the good of that, she says bitterly. But why do you think he's taking their part, I ask her, because I am truly confused. I mean he's a black man. The black woman is clearly in the right, so, as I said before, he can't get into trouble with the company if he tells the white women to get up or get off.

The Somali woman gives me a long look: 'Because he's a slave,' she says. 'He is a slave,' she repeats loudly through the still open back door of the bus, at the driver collecting fares from passengers boarding at the front. I realise from her attitude that they probably already played it all out, she and the women and the driver, before I got on the bus.

'But me,' she says, looking at me hard again, 'I am not a slave. I would rather die than be one.' Her voice is like granite, hard and unmovable. Every word falls heavy as a stone between us, cuts into me like a diamond.

I feel my face turn red as I take Mariam's hand.

All through Mariam's class, that woman's words go round and round in my head. I reckon it's me she's called a slave too, for not sticking up for her. And the thing is, I'm not even mad at her if that's what she's saying. I'm just upset at myself for not doing anything.

And then there's Mariam. People reckon kids forget things quickly. But I know Mariam. All afternoon I sit there watching her. I want to tell her she still shouldn't let people walk all over her, just because they're white, or stronger, or richer, or anything. I don't want her not to stick up for other people if she sees wrong done to them. But I also want to tell her that you can't always do that – you've got to pick your moments. Then I ask myself what's the good of raking it all up again? What's done is done.

After her class, Mariam asks to go to the bagel shop for a hot buttered bagel. This is our usual routine, our little treat. I suggest an extra special treat instead. I take Mariam for a pizza and let her have Coke as extra, extra special. She looks puzzled for a moment at all this, but then she's yakking away, back to her usual bouncy self. I reckon there's nothing like a special treat to let kids forget bad memories. Soon she's blowing bubbles into her Coke through her straw. She's got a smear of pizza tomato on her cheek.

So why can't I forget the whole thing? Is it because I imagine a bit of Mariam's look of this afternoon still about her every time she looks at me?

Romesh Gunesekera

THE LIBRARY

'I AM AFRAID we haven't got a copy, but down in Hornsey they do. Reserve stock. You want me to get it over?'

'Reserve?' Donald raised an eyebrow, bemused.

'Some books are not kept out, you know.'

'But it's only poetry.'

The young librarian laughed. 'It doesn't mean it's pervy. There's just not enough room for everything on the shelves.' She consulted a little card taped to the desk. 'If I call now, it should be here on Wednesday.'

Donald frowned and adjusted his cap; he pulled on a pair of red and yellow knitted gloves. 'No, don't bother. I'll go down there now and ask for it myself. Thank you.'

Donald was a short, dumpy man whose coat was much too big for him. It had belonged to his father. Both his parents had died in the early Thatcher years and he had drifted down to London from Luton with not much more than a bag of old clothes. He had no other family. His father used to talk of an uncle of his who also had come to Britain from Ceylon, like Donald and his parents, but that had been long before the Second World War; he had never kept in touch. As Donald grew older, he became more and more obsessed with information about anyone who could be regarded as a predecessor from the island of his forebears.

Recently he had been on the trail of a poet. He had first caught sight of him in a book about Leonard Woolf; a passing reference to a young Ceylonese poet who had visited the Woolfs in Bloomsbury after the Hogarth Press had reissued *The Village in the Jungle*, the novel Leonard had written after his experience of Ceylon. Donald had first assumed the visitor was Tambimuttu, poet and progressive publisher who was the one of the first to celebrate the new diversity of English poetry. But then he'd discovered that Tambimuttu had arrived in London only in 1938, six years after the reported meeting. Donald had scoured through all the accounts of the 1920s and 1930s he could find, but there was only one other mention of the man. He had been noticed at a bohemian gathering, a glass of cider in his hand, mocking Mr Eliot. 'Tcha, bad move,' Donald had clucked and turned the page. The next sentence simply stated that this fine young poet had gone on to produce one pamphlet — four leaves, seven poems — before disappearing from the scene. Nothing more. No name, no title for the pamphlet, no clue to what had happened. Only that this promising voice had faded away. After that just one minor footnote: there had been a poem apparently dedicated to this Ceylonese writer by a Hornsey poet briefly in the limelight two decades later.

Donald himself was not a poet, although he had flirted with the idea as a young man. To recollect in tranquillity was something he had been prepared to do when he first moved to London. After a few false starts, he had ended up better employed in the downstairs registry of a welfare organisation ordering files from H to P. He had two colleagues dealing with the rest of the alphabet and a boss who drank vodka out of a mug. Donald proved to be a wizard at finding any scrap of paper he filed, but promotion eluded him. Management, he was told after ten years in the department, required more than a prodigious memory and a penchant for paper.

After the initial disappointment of this news, back in 1993, Donald had accepted his limitations and devoted all of his spare time to the preservation of his personal heritage. A man has to find his own place in the scheme of things, he told himself, and began to hoard facts and artefacts from Ceylon, now Sri Lanka, good and bad. His tiny flat on the Archway Road slowly turned into a museum crammed with wooden curios, brassware, files of cuttings and piles of second-hand books of colonial history retrieved from charity shops and bric-a-brac stalls all over London.

On this Saturday morning, it was a little gusty outside the small branch library on Shepherd's Hill. The wind hadn't quite begun to howl as it was doing from Yeovil to Basingstoke, denuding fat oaks and toppling chimney pots, but Donald noticed how it lifted the lids off the bins down the road. He looped his scarf over his cap to keep it in place and made a knot around his neck. He liked his cap – £3.50 from Marker's in Holloway – and he didn't want to lose it.

At the gate, he looked cautiously both ways before stepping out on to the pavement. The last time he had left the library he had been too engrossed in Keynesian economic theory and had blundered into the path of a speeding four-year-old from the nearby community centre. There had been no serious damage but the nap of his suede shoes had not recovered. This time there were no vehicles. Only Janice Conway who was having trouble folding her baby's buggy. The hood billowed like a sail as the wind caught it. Her car door banged shut. 'Oh, bugger,' she swore before she saw Donald.

'Too windy?'

'It's a bloody hurricane.' She put a foot on the buggy's wheel and punched the plastic hood down.

'Can I hold it for you?' Donald asked. He knew her from a neighbourhood residents' meeting, several years earlier, where she had spoken passionately against road-widening. He had seconded her motion and since then they'd exchanged pleasantries on the rare occasions they met.

She was a tall strapping woman and looked down at him from a great height trying to work out which would fly first, the bundle that was Donald, or the rickety buggy. 'If you could hang on to it, I'll strap Tommy in before he leaps out of the other end and creates Armageddon.'

Donald gripped the handle. 'Right. I've got it.'

She yanked the door open again and ducked in; Donald averted his eyes from her stooped back and puckered jeans.

When she emerged again, another gust made him stagger. She caught the buggy and swiftly collapsed it. 'Thanks. Can I give you lift somewhere?'

'It's OK, I am just going down to the main library.'

'Get in. I'll be passing that way. It's not safe walking in this gale.'

Donald looked at the line of trees swaying along the road. The tails of his coat flapped dangerously around his legs. 'Well, if you really are going past it . . .'

'Yes, I am.' She slid behind the wheel and started the car. 'Come on.'

IN THE BACK of the car, Tommy howled and thrashed about. Janice fumbled in an open bag by the gear stick and found a teething ring with brightly coloured plastic keys. She shook it in the air and then, twisting around, passed it to the child. 'Shush, Tommy, shush. Mummy's driving, Tommy, driving.'

Donald noticed that she was looking more in the rear-view mirror than at the road ahead. Perhaps it was inevitable if you crave a family. He checked the buckle of his seat-belt and silently thanked the Romans for their straight roads and the ancients for their ley lines. He had only once before thought of marriage and the idea of bringing up a family. That was when Sharon had joined as the new receptionist at work. She had a lovely smile and her cheerful greeting would always banish his gloom, along with the cold and grime of the street outside. But within three months, before he had plucked up the courage to say anything, she had quit and emigrated to New Zealand with the IT manager on the second floor. Donald had been quite upset.

Tommy howled louder and chucked the teething ring at the window.

'Oh, dear. I'm sorry.' Janice shifted down. Her nose twitched. 'I think he needs a nappy change. I have to pull over. I can't go all the way to Sainsbury's with him like that.' She stopped by the small public garden half-way down the road.

Donald opened the door. 'That's fine. This will do nicely.'

'Why don't you take a turn in the garden. I won't be a minute. Really.'

The wind had dropped and Tommy, awed by his power to stop the car, and his mother, had gone silent. Donald, trapped by a combination of favour and obligation, unnerving social protocol and unpredictable weather, grunted.

He stepped down on to the overgrown path and made his way through the becalmed trees. Above him he heard a woody staccato. He looked up and heard the hammering again, like a highly sprung bouncing ball. Then he saw it: the crested head of an angular woodpecker. He hadn't seen one in years. Not since he'd left Luton. He watched it go again, bobbing madly. Then a big fat pigeon crashed through the trees and the woodpecker flew away. Donald walked down to the empty shambolic field below and gazed at the allotments beyond and the hills on the other side with Alexander Palace shored up like a wreck in the distance. The woods dotted about the hills floated in muted autumn colours. A sense of foreboding seemed to seep out of them, staining the air. He thought of the bird that had vanished. He felt he was becoming invisible too, perhaps like his anonymous poet, lost in a state of hibernation. Besides his colleagues in the basement in Pentonville, the woman at the Post Office, the odd librarian and grocer, and Janice, no one knew him at all and he knew no one else in the city. After Donald's father died, his mother complained that her memories were too much to bear alone. She said she needed more than a graveyard, she needed a sense of a shared past. In Luton they had lived very much on their own.

He made his way slowly back up the path to the car. Janice called out to him. 'That's it. Master Tommy is much happier now.' She handed him a knotted pink polythene bag. 'Could you sling that in the bin for me, please.'

He held it gingerly by one of the loops and dropped it in the black litter bin.

'Nice spot. I sometimes take Tommy down to the field.'

'I saw a woodpecker,' Donald said.

'Blimey. What's it doing here?'

'Nesting?'

Janice tapped a cassette into the car stereo and they set off. 'Yankee Doodle' started and Tommy began to clap his hands.

'Oh, God. Not that.' Janice turned it down.

'He likes it, doesn't he?'

'He loves it. The only bloody thing his father, the ex, ever did was play this. But even that was too much for the tosser.'

Donny nodded. 'It's catchy, but . . .'

'Actually I might pop in with you and pick up a new tape from the kiddies' section. Check out the notice board, too. I find the Hornsey one very handy, don't you?'

'I am looking for a poem.'

'Oh, really?' She turned to look at him, neatly avoiding a flustered masked cyclist as she did so. 'Are you a poet?'

'Not at all.' Donald lowered his head sheepishly. 'I just read a bit.'

'My grandfather was a poet. He wrote a lot of poems back in the fifties. Maybe you know of him? G. F. Parker?'

Donald unwrapped his scarf and pulled off his cap. The car had warmed up with more gleeful tunes and gurgles. 'Parker? That's the one.'

'You are looking for him?' She laughed as she shot through the traffic lights. 'Grandpa?'

Donald gripped the armrest on the door. 'Well, it's this poem you see. He wrote a poem and dedicated it to another poet. That's the one I am looking for.'

'What's his name?'

'That's the problem. All I know is that G. F. Parker dedicated a poem to him. I was going to look for his book to find out.'

'Grandpa was always dedicating poems. How would you know which one?' She took a left turn and a balloon wafted by the window. 'Now, let's hope for a parking space, Tommy. Yell if you see one.'

Tommy squealed at the familiar sign of a party.

'Well done. There we are, just by the nice red postbox.'

She parked and Donald got out of the car. He fitted his cap back on his head while Janice unstrapped the child. Tommy looked up at him and smiled with inexplicable delight.

'You need the . . . pushchair?' Donald asked Janice.

'That's OK. I can carry him in.'

'You say your grandfather dedicated a lot of poems?'

'Hundreds. He loved to make connections. All sorts of famous people he never knew were plonked in. It made him feel good. Part of the scene, you know.'

'Oh.' Donald pondered the prospect of a vast anthology of unclassified names. 'I suppose I'll be able to recognise the name. You see, it was a chap from Ceylon. This poet. And Sri Lankan names are quite easy to spot.'

'You don't mean Rohan, do you? Rohan Amaratunga?'

'Amaratunga?'

'I knew him. He used to come to Grandpa's house when I was little.'

'I am Amaratunga.'

'Obviously not the only one.'

'Rohan, right?' He recalled the name of the uncle his father had talked about. 'A poet?'

'Yes, he wrote a few poems. Later on he wrote a book about the Crimean War. He married Gertie and became very interested in history. OK, Tommy, OK. Stop pulling my ear. Yes, we are going in. Hang on. Now, what was I saying? Rohan's book? We had a copy: a whopping big thing. I gave it, along with a set of Grandpa's poetry books half the size of his, to the library here. You see, they promised to keep an archive of local authors, whatever else they do with videos and computers and what not. A special reserve collection in the basement or somewhere. You should try to see it.'

'I'd like to. Would you?' The words slipped out before he could stop himself.

She looked at him, startled; Tommy saw something in Donald's cap and wriggled towards it. 'OK, OK,' she said, patting the child.

Donald waited for the clamour to subside, for Tommy and Janice, her grandfather and Rohan, to settle in his head, for the next step to become a little clearer.

Max Mueller

A CHAMPION

SO ME AND CARL were chucking stones at Murat's window. We kept missing because he lived four floors up. At last, I hit it with a big one. The clink made us laugh – a little harder and it would have broken the glass. The window opened and out popped Murat's head.

I can't, he said, not tonight. My Dad's gonna be home, and anyway, I'm fasting.

But Carl got out the fag packet, still unopened, and started to take the plastic off, really slowly. We knew Murat wanted a fag badly, because of the fasting. His Dad was strict about it. Carl got the packet open and put the first fag in his mouth, taking his time with the lighter. He lit the fag and for a moment you could see the smile on his face, happy like some wino sucking on a bottle, ahhh, blowing the smoke out in puffs.

Alright then, Murat said, but only for an hour.

His head disappeared, and me and Carl nearly pissed ourselves, the weak bastard, he's gonna be in so much trouble when his Dad gets home. Carl snipped out the fag and put it back in the packet, no use wasting it. After a while the fire door opened and Murat came out, looking left and right just to be sure. He had made a mess of his hair with some wax.

Fag, demanded Murat, snipping his fingers in the direction of the packet.

But Carl looked at Murat's hand full of wax and said, that stuff's disgusting, you'll ruin the fag. You should put that stuff on your trainers, it'll keep the water out.

We started walking and there was some more talk, Murat wanting his fag, it's like we'd cheated him out of the house. Carl said Murat should put the wax on his dick for a smoother wank and Murat said he tried it but the mint made it burn and he couldn't touch it for two days.

What d'you mean, mint, that's what you put on lamb. You mean menthol. We laughed.

So where we going, asked Murat, in a better mood now, the lit cigarette dangling from his mouth, but Carl just flicked his head, meaning you follow me, I'll take you somewhere, you'll see, don't ask questions.

When, really, we all knew we were going to the old elm tree, that's where we always ended up, we just took a different way every time. If you went in a straight line through the estate it would only take about five minutes, but we always went the long way round, checking out the other blocks, walking really slowly. That way we could keep an eye on things.

WE TURNED the corner of Ayer House, and there was no one, and Carl said, have you heard about Sarah Jane, unbelievable.

What, said Murat, what about her?

I couldn't believe it, Carl said. He kept saying it, and Murat kept asking what, what, a little louder every time, until it fucking echoed from the walls. They knew they had me, talking about Sarah Jane. But Carl would not say what it was, and I was glad, although one part of me really wanted to know. It was all lies, anyway. Sarah Jane would never do any of these things. But it made me mad to think, what if she had? Terry had a car, he was older and could talk big. He could talk her into it, and her not knowing any better, because it was her first time. And how nothing I could do afterwards would be as important as the first time, even if I got a car myself. Who remembers the second time, the fifteenth time? Terry, his poxy Honda, even the fucking strawberry-tree air-freshener, she would remember it forever. But even if Carl had told us about Sarah Jane, I wouldn't have heard it. I used to put my hands over my ears like some little kid – lah, lah, lah – but I can do that in my head now, no need for hands, I can go deaf at will.

WE TURNED another corner, and I was relieved, because there were some Peckham girls from Year 9 by the stairs. They pretended not to see us. They laughed really loud the way girls laugh, but you could tell there was nothing funny and it was only to make us look. But we didn't and, as we passed, Murat grabbed hold of the aerial of a parked car, and snapped it off, clean. It made a bang and the girls looked up. Murat is the tallest of us, and taking off that aerial was nothing to him.

What you do that for, shouted one of the girls. That's my Dad's car.

Murat looked kind of lost for a moment, but then said, So? and shrugged his shoulders, not bothered. Carl looked at me, from the corner of his eye.

Yeah, Murat, said Carl, what was that for, and Murat looked a bit annoyed. Her Dad's on the door at Caesar's, you seen him, six foot four, the one with the diamond earring.

So what? I'm not scared of him.

Murat's been going to boxing since he was ten, and he was getting somewhere, Southern Region champion or something. He was going places. Carl and I both went to the gym, but Murat could knock us out any time, no problem. Still, I could tell he was sorry now. Really, he only lived on the next block, and that bouncer guy would come round and see his Dad. So Murat picked up the aerial and tried to shove it back into the hole in the car. Me and Carl were pissing ourselves. Finally, he managed to get it in, kind of crooked. He looked at the girl with the bouncer Dad, a big grin on his face as if he'd just done her a massive favour. But she just stood in front of him with her arms folded. Then the aerial fell off the car again. The bouncer Dad girl started to laugh and all the other girls joined in, shrieking.

Only joking, that's not his car.

You could hardly hear it with the racket they were making. Murat picked up the aerial and went after the girl, who ran off, shrieking some more. He looked like a teacher with a stick in one of the old movies. By now, me and Carl had turned the corner, still laughing.

ACROSS FROM Ayer House was a row of shops. One belonged to Murat's uncle, so we went in. Murat wanted to wait outside because his family doesn't like him mixing with the likes of us. But his uncle saw him and waved, come inside, come inside, with his funny Turkish accent. Me and Carl were flicking through the top shelf magazines but Murat's uncle told us to either buy them or put them back. We were both laughing at some picture, the way the woman was lying must have been really uncomfortable, one leg up in the air, and she was still smiling. Murat's uncle grinned at us, so we put the magazines back and went to the back of the shop to look at the videos. The uncle followed us, and Murat said, Don't worry, Uncle, they won't take anything, they're my friends. There wasn't any porn but Carl found a couple of decent martial arts movies. We talked about some moves I had seen in the cinema, while Murat's uncle was watching us with his grin. I tried hard not to look at him, but you can't help yourself, the harder you try the more difficult it is. So I just stared at the ground. Murat was saying that you would never punch like that, it was a total fake, and Carl went, what, like this? and tried to swing at him. You could see how good Murat really was, because he dodged Carl's shot, fast as lightning, and jabbed him on the chin, lightly, without really hurting him. He was so fast, Carl didn't react at all. We heard this giggle, like from a woman, and it was Murat's uncle.

You still boxing, he said to Murat.

A little.

You're training during Ramadan? That's very hard. Fasting and training, very hard. You must be hungry.

He pushed his hand through the plastic flaps of his fridge unit and grabbed some kind of pie.

I have eaten, Uncle, thank you.

A champion like you must eat. He insisted, Eat, eat, in his funny accent. Me and Carl grinned. Murat was chewing and chewing.

Is something wrong with the pie?

Murat shook his head, no, no, of course not.

Goat cheese, his uncle said, very good for training. When I was a boxer I ate a lot of goat cheese.

You? said Carl, looking at the uncle's belly.

Let's go, said Murat, my Dad's gonna be home.

But the uncle looked at Carl, and at me. I thought of him in the ring with his belly.

I was a boxer, sure, Turkish Junior champion.

Whatever, said Carl. Murat said, sorry Uncle, we have to go, you know what Father's like.

The uncle was kind of puffing his cheeks, Tell your father he must come see me, tell him he has not been to my shop for ages. I want to show your friend something. He puffed his cheeks some more, and raised his fists, jumping up and down, and it made his belly bounce.

You, he said to Carl, I show you. Try hit me.

Carl had to turn away, otherwise he would have burst out laughing. So I said quickly, I'm sorry, Sir, we have to go.

But the uncle was really worked up now, so he didn't notice Carl twisting his face, trying to keep the laughter down. He must have thought we were scared.

I show you kids. I show you.

He said something in Turkish to Murat. Murat said, please, Uncle, we have to go, and took a step towards the doorway.

The uncle skipped over to the door in his boxing mode, and blocked the way. He spoke to Murat in Turkish but Murat looked at the ground, shaking his head.

Go on, Murat, said Carl, he's asking for it.

Murat's face went all red, and he looked from side to side as if to find another exit. But there wasn't one. He jumped forward and brushed past his uncle's belly into the front part of the shop, trying to get out. The uncle was right behind.

I show you, coward, one-two, throwing punches. Me and Carl fell over each other, trying to see. Through the door, Murat in a dead-end aisle, his uncle going for him. He must have landed a punch, because Murat was rubbing his ear. Murat's face was still red, but now there was something else, in his eyes. From where we stood it looked funny, the uncle, short and fat, stamping towards Murat who was rubbing his ear. The uncle took another step, Murat stumbling back, knocking over some mayo glasses, the uncle swinging properly at him. But he was too slow.

Murat dodged the punch, came back up, and landed a hook on his uncle's chin. It was half-hearted, could not even have hurt, but still. The uncle stared for a moment, his mouth open. Then he started screaming in Turkish, and his voice went funny, flipping into a high pitch with every second word. He started hitting Murat, who cowered down with his hands over his head, and the uncle slapped him with his open hand, smacked him like a little boy.

Sorry, Uncle, sorry, and some more in Turkish. Carl went, Oi, stop hitting him, what d'you think you're doing, and he was about to go over and sort the uncle out. But Murat was crying now, he was being beaten like a kid, and crying, and it was strange, somehow we just couldn't help him. But it was all right, the door buzzer went, some customer coming into the shop, and the uncle looked up. I don't think he could have carried on slapping, he was so out of breath. The customer was Baz, the worker from our Youth Club across the road. He came round into the aisle.

Murat got up, wiped his eyes with the back of his hand, and walked past his uncle. He walked fast, past us, past Baz, and said nothing. He was looking at the floor, and there was a little blood coming from his nose. Baz looked at me and Carl, and the mess of the broken mayo glasses, what's going on? Baz knew us and was jumping to conclusions.

Are you all right, Mr Erfat?

Yes, yes, everything all right. The uncle smiled, trying to catch his breath. It's my temper, it's just my temper.

That threw Baz a little, and he was going to call after Murat, but the door buzzer went, he was out of the shop.

Is he all right? Baz asked.

He is fine, fine. He is my nephew. He's fine.

Baz looked at us, You two OK? and we nodded. Baz turned towards the uncle, he was going to say something else. But the uncle had already gone to the back of the shop.

Andrea Levy

LOOSE CHANGE

I AM NOT IN THE HABIT of making friends of strangers. I'm a Londoner. Not even little grey-haired old ladies passing comment on the weather can shame a response from me. I'm a Londoner – aloof sweats from my pores. But I was in a bit of a predicament; my period was two days early and I was caught unprepared.

I'd just gone into the National Portrait Gallery to get out of the cold. It had begun to feel, as I'd walked through the bleak streets, like acid was being thrown at my exposed skin. My fingers were numb, searching in my purse for change for the tampon machine; I barely felt the pull of the zip. But I didn't have any coins. I was forced to ask in a loud voice in this small lavatory, 'Has anyone got three twenty-pence pieces?'

Everyone seemed to leave the place at once – all of them Londoners I was sure of it. Only she was left – fixing her hair in the mirror.

'Do you have change?'

She turned round slowly as I held out a ten-pound note. She had the most spectacular eyebrows. I could see the lines of black hair, like magnetised iron filings, tumbling across her eyes and almost joining above her nose. I must have been staring to recall them so clearly. She had wide black eyes and a round face with such a solid jaw line that she looked to have taken a gentle whack from Tom and Jerry's cartoon frying pan. She dug into the pocket of her jacket and pulled out a bulging handful of money. It was coppers mostly. Some of it tinkled on to the floor. But she had change: too much – I didn't want a bag full of the stuff myself.

'Have you a five-pound note as well?' I asked.

She dropped the coins on to the basin area, spreading them out into the soapy puddles of water that were lying there. Then she said, 'You look?' She had an accent but I couldn't tell then where it was from; I thought maybe Spain.

'Is this all you've got?' I asked. She nodded. 'Well, look, let me just take this now . . .' I picked three damp coins out of the pile. 'Then I'll get some change in the shop and pay them back to you.' Her gaze was as keen as a cat with string. 'Do you understand? Only I don't want all those coins.'

'Yes,' she said softly.

I was grateful. I took the money. But when I emerged from the cubicle the girl and her handful of change were gone.

I found her again staring at the portrait of Darcy Bussell. Her head was inclining from one side to the other as if the painting were a dress she might soon try on for size. I approached her about the money but she just said, 'This is good picture.' Was it my explanation left dangling or the fact that she liked the dreadful painting that caused my mouth to gape?

'Really, you like it?' I said.

'She doesn't look real. It looks like . . .' Her eyelids fluttered sleepily as she searched for the right word, 'a dream.'

That particular picture always reminded me of the doodles girls drew in their rough books at school.

'You don't like?' she asked. I shrugged. 'You show me one you like,' she said.

As I mentioned before, I'm not in the habit of making friends of strangers, but there was something about this girl. Her eyes were encircled with dark shadows so that even when she smiled – introducing herself cheerfully as Laylor – they remained as mournful as a glum kid at a party. I took this fraternisation as defeat but I had to introduce her to a better portrait.

Alan Bennett with his mysterious little brown bag didn't impress her at all. She preferred the photograph of Beckham. Germaine Greer made her top lip curl and as for A. S. Byatt, she laughed out loud, 'This is child make this?'

We were almost making a scene. Laylor couldn't keep her voice down and people were beginning to watch us. I wanted to be released from my obligation. 'Look, let me buy us both a cup of tea,' I said. 'Then I can give you back your money.'

She brought out her handful of change again as we sat down at a table – eagerly passing it across to me to take some for the tea.

'No, I'll get this,' I said.

Her money jangled like a win on a slot machine as she tipped it back into her pocket. When I got back with the tea, I pushed over the twenty-pences I owed her. She began playing with them on the tabletop – pushing one around the other two in a figure of eight. Suddenly she leant towards me as if there were a conspiracy between us and said, 'I like art.' With that announcement a light briefly came on in those dull eyes to reveal that she was no more than eighteen. A student perhaps.

'Where are you from?' I asked.

'Uzbekistan,' she said.

Was that the Balkans? I wasn't sure. 'Where is that?'

She licked her finger, then with great concentration drew an outline on to the tabletop. 'This is Uzbekistan,' she said. She licked her finger again to carefully plop a wet dot on to the map saying, 'And I come from here – Tashkent.'

'And where is all this?' I said, indicating the area around the little map with its slowly evaporating borders and town. She screwed up her face as if to say nowhere.

'Are you on holiday?' I asked.

She nodded.

'How long are you here for?'

Leaning her elbows on the table she took a sip of her tea. 'Ehh, it is bitter!' she shouted.

'Put some sugar in it,' I said, pushing the sugar sachets toward her.

She was reluctant, 'Is for free?' she asked.

'Yes, take one.'

The sugar spilled as she clumsily opened the packet. I laughed it off but she, with the focus of a prayer, put her cup up to the edge of the table and swept the sugar into it with the side of her hand. The rest of the detritus that was on the tabletop fell into the tea as well. Some crumbs, a tiny scrap of paper and a curly black hair floated on the surface of her drink. I felt sick as she put the cup back to her mouth.

'Pour that one away, I'll get you another one.'

Just as I said that a young boy arrived at our table and stood, legs astride, before her. He pushed down the hood on his padded coat. His head was curious – flat as a cardboard cut-out – with hair stuck to his sweaty forehead in black curlicues. And his face was as doggedly determined as two fists raised. They began talking in whatever language it was they spoke. Laylor's tone pleading – the boy's aggrieved. Laylor took the money from her pocket and held it up to him. She slapped his hand away when he tried to wrest all the coins from her palm. Then, as abruptly as he had appeared, he left.

Laylor called something after him. Everyone turned to stare at her, except the boy, who just carried on.

'Who was that?'

With the teacup resting on her lip, she said, 'My brother. He want to know where we sleep tonight.'

'Oh, yes, where's that?' I was rummaging through the contents of my bag for a tissue, so it was casually asked.

'It's square we have slept before.'

'Which hotel is it?' I thought of the Russell Hotel, that was on a square with uniformed attendants, bed turning-down facilities, old-world style.

She was picking the curly black hair off her tongue when she said, 'No hotel, just the square.'

It was then I began to notice things I had not seen before: dirt under each of her chipped fingernails, the collar of her blouse crumpled and unironed, a tiny cut on her cheek, a fringe that looked to have been cut with blunt nail-clippers. I found a tissue and used it to wipe my sweating palms.

'How do you mean just in the square?'

'We sleep out in the square,' she said. It was so simple she spread her hands to suggest the lie of her bed.

'Outside?'

She nodded.

'Tonight?'

'Yes.'

The memory of the bitter cold still tingled at my fingertips as I said, 'Why?' It took her no more than two breaths to tell me the story. She and her brother had had to leave their country, Uzbekistan, when their parents, who were journalists, were arrested. It was arranged very quickly – friends of their parents acquired passports for them and put them on to a plane. They had been in England for three days but they knew no one here. This country was just a safe place. Now all the money they had could be lifted in the palm of a hand to a stranger in a toilet. So they were sleeping rough – in the shelter of a square, covered in blankets, on top of some cardboard.

At the next table a woman was complaining loudly that there was too much froth on her coffee. Her companion was relating the miserable tale of her daughter's attempt to get into publishing. What did they think about the strange girl sitting opposite me? Nothing. Only I knew what a menacing place Laylor's world had become. She'd lost a tooth. I noticed the ugly gap when she smiled at me saying, 'I love London.'

She had sought me out – sifted me from the crowd. This young woman was desperate for help. She'd even cunningly made me obliged to her.

'I have picture of Tower Bridge at home on wall although I have not seen yet.'

But why me? I had my son to think of. Why pick on a single mother with a young son? We haven't got the time. Those two women at the next table, with their matching hand-bags and shoes, they did nothing but lunch. Why hadn't she approached them instead?

'From little girl, I always want to see it . . .' she went on.

I didn't know anything about people in her situation. Didn't they have to go somewhere? Croydon, was it? Couldn't she have gone to the police? Or some charity? My life was hard enough without this stranger tramping through it. She smelt of mildewed washing. Imagine her dragging that awful stink into my kitchen. Cupping her filthy hands round my bone china. Smearing my white linen. Her big face with its pantomime eyebrows leering over my son. Slumping on to my sofa and kicking off her muddy boots as she yanked me down into her particular hell. How would I ever get rid of her?

'You know where is Tower Bridge?'

Perhaps there was something tender-hearted in my face. When my grandma first came to England from the Caribbean she lived through days as lonely and cold as an open grave. The story she told all her grandchildren was about the stranger who woke her while she was sleeping in a doorway and offered her a warm bed for the night. It was this act of benevolence that kept my grandmother alive. She was convinced of it. Her Good Samaritan.

'Is something wrong?' the girl asked.

Now my grandmother talks with passion about scrounging refugees; those asylum seekers who can't even speak the language, storming the country and making it difficult for her and everyone else.

'Last week . . .' she began, her voice quivering, 'I was in home.' This was embarrassing. I couldn't turn the other way, the girl was staring straight at me. 'This day, Friday,' she went on, 'I cooked fish for my mother and brother.' The whites of her eyes were becoming soft and pink; she was going to cry. 'This day Friday I am here in London,' she said. 'And I worry I will not see my mother again.'

Only a savage would turn away when it was merely kindness that was needed. I resolved to help her. I had three warm bedrooms, one of them empty. I would make her dinner. Fried chicken or maybe poached fish in wine. I would run her a bath filled with bubbles. Wrap her in thick towels heated on a rail. I would then hunt out some warm clothes and after I had put my son to bed I would make her cocoa. We would sit and talk. I would let her tell me all that she had been through. Wipe her tears and assure her that she was now safe. I would phone a colleague from school and ask him for advice. Then in the morning I would take Laylor to wherever she needed to go.

And before we said goodbye I would press my phone number into her hand.

All Laylor's grandchildren would know my name.

Her nose was running with snot. She pulled down the sleeve of her jacket to drag it across her face and said, 'I must find my brother.'

I didn't have any more tissues. 'I'll get you something to wipe your nose,' I said.

I got up from the table. She watched me, frowning; the tiny hairs of her eyebrows locking together like Velcro. I walked to the counter where serviettes were lying in a neat pile. I picked up four. Then standing straight I walked on. Not back to Laylor but up the stairs to the exit. I pushed through the revolving doors and threw myself into the cold.

Alex Wheatle

SHADE-ISM

'LATE AREN'T YOU?' barked Monica, greeting her husband at the front door with her hands on her hips, seizing him with an accusing stare. Her eyes were puffy and her voice was desperate. 'Sure you weren't giving dictation to dat Jody bitch?'

'What you chatting 'bout,' answered Horace, brushing past his wife and hanging his coat in the hallway. He knew he had been caught in a lie but wanted to act normal to refute his wife's suspicions.

'Don't fucking take me for a rarse fool, I know so you been screwing her!' Monica raised her voice, her husband's indifference fuelling her anger.

Horace, his face full of apathy, made his way to the lounge, heading for the TV. He switched it on to the Sky sports channel as Monica huffed in swift pursuit. He sat down on the sofa. Two carved African masks and a black-and-white monochrome painting of a slave ship were hanging on the wall, providing a backdrop for the television. Monica was proud of recognising her roots.

'You're too para, man,' Horace countered, his eyes glued on the TV. 'It's like you never forgive me for dat mistake ah couple ah year back.'

'Mistake? *Mistakes* you lying wretch. You don't remember dat red-skin bitch after Clayton's stag night?'

Horace threw his hands in the air. 'Everyone knows I was drunk up dat night. You can't include dat cos I didn't know what I was doing . . . And she was brown-skin – not as light-skinned as you're making out.'

'You had nuff of your senses to put your t'ing in her stinkin' pussy,' Monica replied, looming threateningly over her husband's shoulder.

Horace turned the volume up on the TV then wrenched off his tie. 'I don't need dis, man. Come home from work an' all you can do is go para on me 'bout some girl at work an' bring up de past. You're always striking me wid dat stick . . . An' where are de kids?'

Monica patrolled around the back of the cream leather sofa where her husband was sitting. Her eyes bore the evidence of bottled-up rage that she couldn't cap any longer and her breathing up-tempoed near to an asthma attack. 'Der at my Mum's. Didn't want dem witnessing dat der fader t'inks more of his dick dan his family!'

Horace stood up and faced his wife over the settee. He was taken aback by his wife's fury and knew he had to calm the situation. He hadn't seen her like this before, even when his other affairs were discovered. 'Oh, for God's sake. As usual you're blowing dis up outta proportion. Me an' Jody are nutten but friends an' sometimes we go to lunch together, dat's all.'

'You mus' t'ink I'm a fucking idiot. I phoned up Darren last night, remember him, you said you was going to check him last night. You weren't fucking der, Horace. Where de fuck was you?'

'So you're checking up on me. Dat's trust for you.'

'Where de fuck were you last night?'

'I ain't taking dis. Cha! Craziness is taking you.'

Horace marched to the stairs and bounded up them, shaking his head. His steps reverberated all over the house as Monica kissed her teeth, banging her fists against the sofa. Anticipating for the truth to emerge, she slowly followed her husband to the marital bedroom. She found Horace looking through his CDs. 'Why can't you jus' admit it. When it comes to the trut' you're jus' a mouse.'

'Alright den!' Horace yelled, flinging the CDs all over the bed. 'Yeah, I did. You fucking happy now. I fucked Jody, right! Is dat what you wanted to hear?'

'You fucking dick-happy bastard.' Monica picked up one of her shoes and threw it with intent, aimed for her husband's head. 'Good was she? A few years younger dan me is she? Ain't got no stretch marks has she? You can fuck off out of de yard an' take yourself to her yard.'

Monica jumped on her husband, slapping him about the head as tears rolled down her cheeks. 'I should fuckin' bruk dat t'ing between your legs.' Horace grabbed her arms and realised the deep hurt he had caused. Monica tried to free her wrists and lashed out with her feet, kicking Horace on the back of his head. She also managed to claw him under the chin, drawing a fine line of blood. Horace was surprised by the strength of his wife, but he was six foot plus with weight to match. He threw her off the bed where she toppled over the bedside cabinet and the clock radio that was upon it. 'Why!' she screamed. 'Why?'

Horace refused to answer and avoided looking at his wife as she composed herself, realising she was no match for a fight with her husband. She found her cigarettes and lighter on the dressing table next to a small framed photo of her and her husband on their wedding day. 'Let me guess,' she said, igniting her cancer stick, her voice falling into a sarcastic zone.

'Red-skin was she? Or a browning as you like to call them. Like de other two who I know you've cheated wid. Don't you like a black-skin girl? Don't you like your own fuckin' colour? Cos you're black like de inside of a non-stick pan, jus' like me. Why de fuck did you marry me if you wanna screw red-skin bitches all de while. Why, Horace? Makes you feel good does it? Maybe we should have decorated the house in fuckin' red, then you might feel at home, to rarted. It's like you enjoy hurting me. Maybe you wanted me to find out, jus' to make me feel like shit, innit.'

Horace turned his back to his wife and looked out the window, feeling his wife's pain. He didn't mean to hurt her, he thought. He couldn't understand the reason why he craved sex with other available women. They were willing and he had accepted. Their lighter shade of brown was just a coincidence. 'I didn't do it to hurt you,' he finally replied.

'Den why, Horace? We have a nice yard, an' we've never had a problem in bed. We have two nice kids. Tell me why cos I'm freaking out t'inking what I might have done wrong. An' believe, I t'ought 'bout it for hours, an' I ain't done nutten to you to deserve dis shit.'

'It's not you.'

Monica glanced across the bed, and through the mist of her cigarette smoke, noted her husband's eyes were staring at the carpet in genuine sorrow. His nineteen-inch neck was supported by a back that a cruiserweight would have been proud of. Nuff women must desire him, Monica thought. 'What d'you mean? If you had respect for me den you wouldn't screw other bitches.'

'It's nutten to do wid you,' Horace insisted. 'I've always respected you.'

'An' dis is how you show your respect?'

'Cha! You don't understand.'

'Don't fucking understand! So I'm s'posed to understand dat you go round screwing other women. Do you know how I feel? You make me feel like I'm a wort'less woman who can't give her man what he wants.'

'I don't mean it like dat.'

'I cook you a fucking meal every day. You've always got a clean shirt in de morning an' you always come home to a clean yard. I tend to de kids every day, an' I even bring in a liccle money from my part-time job to help out. But dat ain't fucking good enough for you. *Is* it? You have to fuck about wid some bitch at work.'

Horace stretched out his hand to turn on the mini-stereo and inserted a CD. Luciano's *It's Me Again Jah* emitted from the shoe-box-size speakers. A framed picture of Marcus Garvey, appearing immensely proud in his black skin, was hanging over the top of the bed, looking down on the both of them. Monica had bought it. It made her feel good to have this sort of thing around her house.

'So what?' continued Monica. 'Don't wanna hear what I have to say? Tryin' to drown me out. You ain't gettin' away wid dis so easy, an' you might as well pack your fuckin' bags cos you ain't staying here tonight.'

Turning off the stereo, Horace went downstairs to the kitchen. Monica abruptly killed her cigarette on the dressing table ashtray, then hounded after her husband again. She found him peering into the fridge, contemplating on what to eat. 'If you t'ink I'm cooking for you again you're making a sad mistake.'

'Can't you shut de fuck up! You've made your point.'

'Shut up? You've got a fuckin' rarse cheek telling me to shut up. You should have said dat to your desires when you screwed dat Jody bitch. Does she always screw married men? Serial husband-shagger is she? Goes on like she's better dan dark-skin women does she?'

'Fuck dis,' yelled Horace, slamming the fridge door and throwing his arms up in the air. 'I'm going round my Mum's.'

'Well fuckin' mek sure you don't tek a detour to Jody's yard. Wouldn't surprise me if de red bitch is in your fuckin' car, waiting for you to come out.'

'She ain't light-skin,' affirmed Horace. 'She's white!'

A festering anger that had taken residence within Monica took over all of her senses. Her breathing bordered on hyper-ventilation and the gums around her teeth slowly exposed themselves. Her nostrils flared as her bottom lip danced. She grabbed the bread knife which hung over the sink, which was full of unwashed cutlery. Horace saw his peril, the whites of his eyes crudely expanding, and raised his arms to defend himself. With a manic lunge, the knife missed Horace's right arm and pierced him with a crazed force under his armpit. The tip of the blade protruded out of his breast, just missing his nipple.

The look on Horace's features was of disbelief as his giant frame crashed to the floor, with his head kissing the cooker on the way down.

Inhaling almost fatally, Monica dropped the knife from her trembling hand and backed away, hypnotised by the blood that was forming a neat puddle underneath her husband's shoulder, his sky-blue shirt changing colour before her eyes. His head shook a little before this movement died and his shocked eyes closed. Monica gaped at the blood on her fingers, then her eyes moved to the black skin that covered her hand. But the only colour she saw before her was red.

Saeed Taji Farouky

THE RAIN MISSED MY FACE AND FELL STRAIGHT TO MY SHOES

I'M LOOKING FOR CHANGE in my pocket, flicking through the coins all one- and two-pence pieces. I'm trying to make up at least two pounds with all the spare coins because Faris said he can't let me into the theatre any more for free. Otherwise his boss is going to get suspicious and Faris would maybe lose his job so I have to give him some change. I turn over everything I have, which is only eighty-seven pence anyway. He starts counting the coins and I can see it isn't going to be enough. People are behind me in the queue, getting impatient. Faris looks behind him in the booth, then to me, 'It's not even a pound, Samir.'

I have to lean down to speak quietly through the gap in the glass, 'I know. I don't have enough. It's OK for now, isn't it?'

'Just go inside, there are other people waiting. I don't have time to argue now.' Faris is scowling, trying not to look me in the eyes. But there's a familiarity we have that means he understands me by now, he knows that I always do this. Faris piles the coins next to the ticket machine and yells for the next person in line.

I used to feel guilty when I tried to get into Faris's theatre for free, but not any more, not since I started letting him on to the tube for nothing – not even one or two pounds. I walk with my ticket into the foyer and look for someone else I recognise.

I know it'll either be Youssef or Hamza. Youssef is Egyptian so he gets along well with me. Hamza is I think from Somalia – we don't have much in common; not much. He can't speak English very well, or Arabic, so we can only have very simple conversations about his family. I can tell that Hamza doesn't like me coming in to the cinema, and he's worried about his job as well, but he doesn't know that *everyone* lets their friends in for free – even the boss and the English people working here. That's why I prefer it when Youssef is at the gate because he knows that there's nothing to worry about.

This time it's Youssef and he smiles and puts out his arms for a hug when he sees me. His hairy arms tickle my neck when he leans in to hug me. He has a thin beard that pricks my face. The other customers in the queue turn to look at us, two men hugging, but Youssef doesn't care. He's a very private man, but somehow he never seems afraid if people notice him. He's never afraid to let people stare at him and wonder who he is. I'm the opposite: I always get anxious when people look at me; I try to make out their reactions to everything I do. I worry they're looking for something that isn't really in me, but if they look hard enough, they might see it anyway. I'm smiling when Youssef hugs me because I haven't seen him in more than two weeks. I'm usually at the cinema every day, sometimes a few times a day.

'Samir! You son of a bitch!'

'Don't swear so loud, people will hear you.' Youssef is hugging me with one hand and tearing tickets with the other. People have to step around us to get through the gate.

'Where were you, I haven't seen you in weeks. Hamza says you haven't been, either.'

'No, I was visiting my Mum, she was sick in hospital. I had to go stay with her in hospital.'

'Your Mum was sick? I didn't know. I'm sorry.' He takes back his arm from around me and steps to the side to tear someone else's ticket. I can see everyone else is getting impatient because he's ignoring them and not telling anyone their screen number. Some people are trying to listen to our conversation. Youssef smiles to his customers as he's talking to me: 'I hope she's OK now, huh?'

'No, she died.' Some more people get their tickets torn and walk past us through the gates. We both stand beside each other for a few moments in silence. Customers pass by. Youssef doesn't look at me but puts one hand on my shoulder and is trying to say something sensible while he's tearing the tickets. I finally have to move out of the way to let the other customers through, and his hand falls from my shoulder. I give him a few seconds to think of something to say, but I don't want to make him uncomfortable, with the customers all standing around us, I don't want to embarrass him. 'I'll see you after the film, Youssef . . .'

'No, I'll see you in there,' he says to me. 'I'm coming in now.' Youssef looks over his shoulder to the far end of the foyer. The toilet door swings open, and I see Hamza clumsily pushing his way out carrying a mop in one hand and bucket in the other. Youssef tries to wave him over, but Hamza doesn't see him. He's just finished the day's third cleaning, mopping up all the shit and piss and disgusting things people leave behind in cheap toilets when they don't care about them. I used to do that job as well, anyone who works in the cinema has to do all the jobs – except Hamza who doesn't sell or tear tickets because of his English. When he sees Youssef waving, he carefully puts the mop and bucket into the service closet and walks over. His dark black skin shines blue under the halogen lights of the foyer, thin arms pressed tightly to his sides and hands forced into his pockets. Youssef asks Hamza to tear the tickets in his place, and Hamza says OK because Youssef has a personality that makes people want to do what he says. He doesn't push, but he always manages to convince you that his ideas are clever or sensible. While I was working there, he always got me to count the money at the end of the night, which was the worst job, and no one wanted to do it because it was so boring and you were always the last to leave. He also managed to convince me, every Friday night, to take a few pounds from the till and go drinking with him. I never wanted to steal and I didn't drink before I worked there but Youssef made me want to do all of that.

He takes my arm and walks me through the swinging doors and into one of the theatres, looking for spaces at the back right, under the balcony. That's where you always find the people who got in for free or people who just snuck in or people who paid for one ticket in the morning and stayed in the cinema all day moving from film to film, sometimes sleeping behind the seats if no one saw them. Youssef and I take the empty seats behind two boys I recognise, two boys that I always see here. They sit next to each other and pass a mobile phone between them, sometimes both talking on it, sometimes just writing messages. Next to us, there's one Arab or Iranian man who is a bit older than me and has a beard and looks like a religious man, but I always see him drinking cans of beer in his seat. He's sitting next to the air conditioner vent. I see one black guy who once brought a prostitute in, or maybe not a prostitute but a girl who didn't mind doing things in a cinema and that's what they did. I also see a fat white man who usually sits a few rows ahead and at the end of the film always asks Youssef and me and anyone else I'm with, 'What did you boys think of *that*?' Especially when it's a film about

war: 'What did you boys think of *that*?' with his arms waving
and the loose skin billowing. There are some other people
around but I don't recognise them. Everyone else, the real
customers, are sitting further up so they can see the screen.
Back here no one cares if we talk because they're not here to
see the film anyway, so Youssef and I talk and he asks me what
happened to my mother and I tell him.

I tell him that she was in Cairo when she got sick and they
wanted her to go to hospital there, but no one could pay for it.
So they thought she could get treated in London for free, but
of course they had to pay for the plane ticket and still no one
had the money. My family tried to put everything they had
together but it still wasn't enough, and at the same time my
cousin was having a baby so they needed that money. That's
when I stole the whole day's till from the cinema, and with that
I bought the plane ticket. The next day I lost my job. All this
Youssef knew. But since my Mum made it to London, that was
seventeen days ago, I hadn't seen him or been to the cinema at
all. I was staying with my Mum in hospital. At midnight I
would go to work in the underground stations until 8 a.m.,
then I could go back to the hospital.

'After seventeen days she died. It was very slow. And I have
to spend all my money again to send her body back to Cairo. I
can't even go with her. I have to look for another job.' I'm
trying to raise my voice above the sounds of the screaming
coming from the film. It's a film about a woman who finds out
her daughter is being followed by a killer, that's what I understand so far, and the woman now is trying to find out who the
killer is and what he wants with her daughter. Youssef says in
Arabic the things that we will always say when someone dies,
that is, 'She will live on inside you,' and 'God have mercy on
you,' and 'God give you good health.' These things we never

really have to think about because they are phrases already written by generations and hundreds of years of people's parents dying. Generations of killing children and starving and being murdered in the name of God. We can recite the phrases and then forget about the death and move on. I know Youssef won't forget, but it always sounds shallow when someone uses these phrases. And the person grieving knows those words all sound empty and insincere but there's nothing anyone can do about it. We keep using them.

The killer turns out to be someone the mother knows and now she's chasing him across the city. There's a policeman with her, and the policeman's father was shot before when he was also a policeman.

'Samir, I know someone who can do it properly here, who can do a Muslim funeral here.'

'No, she's supposed to be buried in Cairo. Everyone there is waiting for me to send her but I don't have the money. I need money.' It reminds me of when I would break something in my grandmother's house. The place was filled with antiques and whenever we went to visit, when I was younger, I would always break something. She would tell me it was all right as long as I paid for it, and I would say 'Later,' but I never did pay for anything.

'I don't have anything I can give you.' Youssef is talking to me but looking straight ahead, his eyes on the screen.

'I wasn't expecting anything from you.' I turn my head to face him. 'That's not what I meant. I just wanted to tell you.' Now the woman and the policeman find the killer just before he reaches the daughter. The daughter doesn't know he's after her. The policeman gets shot and dies before the killer falls from the roof or from a balcony. The lights come up and everyone slides from out of their chairs and throws empty boxes and cups on the floor and the fat white man sees us and his eyes get wide. 'Well, what did you boys think of *that*?' He crosses his arms over his belly and looks at both of us with relish, waiting for a reply, but I'm not going to say anything. Youssef finally offers this: 'I think the girl was stupid, she should have known he was coming to kill her!' The fat man nods his head, 'I was thinking that as well,' and smiles broadly to himself as he limps out of the cinema with the other customers.

WHEN I STOLE the money from the cinema, everyone else said they wouldn't tell the boss it was me. They knew it was me because I'd been talking about it for a few days, but all of us working there stayed together and usually let the rest of the staff get away with whatever they were doing. No one wants to cause any problems for themselves, and the best way to avoid that is to do your job. Don't say anything if you aren't asked. We're all illegal so no point in bringing trouble on all of us. They said they wouldn't tell the boss who it was but everyone knew and someone must have said something in the end because the boss told me straight, the next morning, that I didn't have a job there any more. But that didn't bother me, because I had already taken the money the night before and hidden it in my flat. Now I think it would have been better if I had just taken the money for myself. Just kept it. My mother died anyway, better for her to have died in Cairo with the family and then be buried there straight away. I say that to Youssef but he tries to make me feel better and says, 'There was no way to know, was there? You couldn't have known. You did what you could.' Now I have to go through losing her and losing all the money at the same time.

As Youssef and I walk out of the cinema, Hamza follows to tell us something. He's trying to give us a message, but he's difficult to understand because of his English. Youssef and I eventually figure out that the message has to do with the boss; he says I can't come to the cinema any more since I lost my job. If he sees my here again he'll call the police and have me arrested. Youssef laughs because he laughs when he's nervous. My face is straight, I don't have the energy to react. When Hamza says the word 'police', I imagine the policeman from the film. I imagine him chasing me in a taxi and getting shot before I fall off a roof. Now I'll have to find somewhere else to waste hours of every day. Somewhere else dark to hide in when I can't bear to go back to the flat and I can't afford a proper meal. I'll have to find somewhere else to buy my hashish from.

THE NEXT NIGHT I meet Youssef outside the cinema when he's done working, and he brings Aqil with him, a friend from Iraq. Aqil was in the army there but he thought because he had a doctorate degree in physics he shouldn't be in the army. So the government said he could work on their physics programme, but he escaped to come to England instead. Aqil is short and very wide, now he wears thick glasses and has his hair combed over the top. When he was younger he was very handsome – he showed me a picture of himself when he was a weight-lifter. He also used to be on the National Weight-Lifting Team, then he came to London and started working in a video shop. He watches the news all day on the shop's television even though he's supposed to play the new films.

We walk to a café not far from the cinema, on one of the smaller streets behind Charing Cross Road. There's a Turkish guy who runs the place, they sell fish and chips and pies. Aqil sits facing me and looks into his cup of coffee for a few minutes before starting with, 'Samir, can you believe Blair? He is such a fool! I'm serious, he is a fool if he thinks he can control Iraq like this: Be democratic . . .' he lays down his coffee and holds his two hands up as though he's aiming a rifle at my chest '. . . or I'll kill you. This is his foreign policy.' I look down at his fingers pointed to my chest. That's how our conversations always begin, then we go on from there insulting European and American leaders. At some point in every conversation Aqil will say, 'And don't forget, it's really our fault. We let them push us around like this . . .' and no one's satisfied by the end of it. I once saw Aqil crying when they were showing on TV pictures of people in Iraq, men on the streets of Baghdad, stealing things from the National Museum and smashing everything to pieces. The city and the windows and someone's car and banks and people's houses, all being taken to bits. 'Those statues', he said, pointing to images of stolen antiques on the screen, 'were made when Europeans were still running around in the mud! Living in caves!'

I drink my third coffee and Aqil asks about my mother. He must have heard from someone else that she was sick. I don't say anything, but Youssef shakes his head and waves a finger at Aqil. We talk about marriage instead. I've been thinking about it for months now, but I haven't met anyone I love. We decide maybe I don't have to wait to find someone I love. Then on the TV there are pictures of piles of dead bodies but I can't tell if they're American or Iraqi. We've been sitting in the café for two and a half hours by now, waiting for our night shifts to start. I can see girls walking past outside – girls dressed up to go out with their friends, girls in suits on their way back from work (maybe they have to work late or they're sleeping with the boss), girls already drunk, girls who look scared to walk in the streets alone, girls who look really ill and they're trying to find someone to pay them for sex. While looking out the door, looking at the girls passing, I ask Aqil if he knows where I can get some money. I carefully ask, 'What about you, do you have any money I can borrow?' He has his fingers locked together, resting on the table, and he opens his hands to answer with enthusiasm, 'If I knew where to get money, I would get it!' and Youssef and I laugh with him. It's pathetic and we know it's true but we laugh with him. Everyone is always looking for ways to make money. I once went round to people in the streets with a stolen stereo and tried to persuade someone to buy it, but no one would even talk to me. I didn't steal it but the man who stole it asked me to sell it for him and said I could keep some of the money. I hated to think of myself as a criminal. I thought if I stayed far away from the guy who stole it, if I didn't get close to him, I would be fine. I mean, I would still be clean. But it didn't work and I couldn't sell the stereo and I still felt like a thief. That made me sick. Aqil would often say about himself, 'I left my country to escape from criminals and I came here, and I became a criminal!' That's how I felt with the stereo. But Aqil reads a lot and watches the news all day so he always thinks too much about what he's going through. Youssef and I try not to think about it; we go to the cinema and watch films instead.

AQIL COMES IN to see me one night when I'm working in the kitchen of Café Tangier. I got the job from someone Youssef knows who used to be in the military in Egypt. His father was something like a captain under King Farouk and he had to leave the country with the king during the revolution. Youssef's friend got me a job serving tables at the Tangier and that was good money. Sometimes I could overcharge tourists, or foreigners who had just arrived in London, by one or two pounds and they wouldn't notice because they couldn't read the menu. But I can't serve in the restaurant any more after the police came and found me and some Hungarian girls working without papers. So I moved to the kitchen. I can still work in the kitchen and probably no one will find me there. That's what I mean by feeling like a criminal. I'm not doing anything illegal, I'm only trying to make a living. Washing up in a kitchen, my family wouldn't believe it. That would be a disgrace. That's why I don't tell them what I'm doing. I tell them instead that I'm doing fine and I'm happy and making money. I can't tell them I came to London to become a criminal. When I look at myself, I don't see a criminal. I don't see a good man. All I want is to live simply. I don't want to get rich, suck the money out of this country. No one would believe that, they don't imagine that at all. I want to tell them, 'I'm only trying to earn a living. You have to work too – I'm just working.' That's what it's like in the kitchen.

Aqil comes by to tell me there's a car coming in from France. His cousin is coming to London for the weekend to meet him and pick up a few days of work building around Holland Park. There are a lot of rich Arabs in Holland Park who pay to have work done. Some of them prefer to have other Arabs working for them. Some people say it's because they want to give back to the poorer ones in London, to show their appreciation, but I think it's because they want to be reminded of what things were like for them at home, when they had servants and maids.

'We can go with them to Paris. It's my cousin who moved to Syria, he speaks French.'

'What would we do there?'

'We could find something else there. My brother can help us find work.'

'What kind of work?'

'I don't know. He says it's better than here.'

But I don't speak French. I don't know Paris at all. By now

I'm used to where things are in London: where the money is, where there are jobs going and which ones are safe. That takes a lot of time to learn. I stand over the sink, with Aqil next to me hovering like he's waiting for an answer right now. He's sitting on the counter and his legs don't touch the floor. I stop washing and hold my hands down to let some of the soap drip from my fingers. My shirt was white, now it's grey, spattered with water from the sink. I'm thinking about Paris and what it must look like at night compared to London, whether it also has a Soho with mini-cabs and empty beer cans and girls who look sick and counting the money in the till until midnight. And mothers coming over because they have no money and dying in the city.

I hear Aqil's voice mumbling, but I don't hear the words clearly. I look over and see his lips moving with the same sound but I don't hear his voice. I hear the words to an old song, one where the diva sings, 'The world is a cigarette and a drink, when people abandon you . . .' and her voice moans with the floating sound of the strings. Most people would say she means the cigarette and the drink are all you have left. But I always thought she was saying that everywhere you can see chances. Everywhere you see little insignificant things that can comfort you. Maybe it's a drink or a cigarette or a girl but when everything is lost, you find suddenly there are little pieces everywhere that give you hope, more hope than when things were going well. You can see hope in everything. This is what I'm hearing until Aqil jumps down from the counter and brushes his hands on his trousers. He starts to look apologetic as he turns to walk out of the kitchen. He pauses before the door to say, 'Youssef is coming with me,' and that's the sound of the orchestra rising in a crescendo. I know I'll be alone if I decide not to go with them. I couldn't stand being alone. I turn to face Aqil and he can see on my face what I'm thinking: that I'm afraid to be alone. That I'm afraid to go to Paris. This is like everything else that controls me.

I leave the restaurant early. There aren't many customers anyway so I'll finish washing in the morning. I stand in the doorway and I see the rain hitting the pavement in some spots where it's lit orange by the street lamps. I remember then that I still have a hole in my left shoe, where the sole is split, and if I walk out like this the water's going to soak through my sock and get my foot wet. I'm feeling sick now, sick in my stomach like I'm hungry or I have a hangover but I can't get rid of the sensation. Even when I eat something. I'm just sick thinking of what Aqil mentioned. The idea of going to Paris. I buy four cans of cheap beer from the newsagent's and I open the first one just as I'm stepping on to the tube to get me out of Stoke Newington and all the way down to south London where I can hide behind the warehouses and factories. My foot is already soaking wet. I wish I could have done something like the man who escaped from Egypt with King Farouk. I could be running from something dangerous – that would be honourable. But I'm just running around looking for spare jobs and trying to avoid the police. If I was in exile with the king, no one would look at me like I was a criminal. I could say, 'I did it for my country,' or, 'I did it for my king,' and it would be glorious. English people would understand that's something you have to do, to save your king, and that would be a good reason to be on the run or to be afraid all the time. That would be a good reason to hide my money and buy four cans of beer every once in a while and drink them on my own. Or a good reason to bring your mother over and watch her die, because that's how people in exile have to live. My family could be angry at me but they couldn't be ashamed of me because everyone would know I did it for my country first, and I was willing to die for my country. But I didn't die and I escaped to London. That's my fantasy.

I'm still feeling sick on the tube, and people are watching me now drinking my beer and still wearing my dirty clothes from work. In front of me is a girl sleeping with her head resting on the glass. I can still see the oil from other people's hair smeared on the glass but the girl doesn't seem to notice. She's very young, the girl, and starting to look pretty. I scratch my back through my shirt. Then I have to reach under my shirt to scratch the skin properly, with my nails. The girl opens her eyes while I'm still looking at her, but I forget to smile. She quickly shuts her eyes again, pretending to sleep. I don't know what else to say to her, except, 'I had to escape from the revolution. They were going to kill me if I didn't escape, because I wanted to save my king. Because I love my king.' I only say that because I'm a little drunk by now. Otherwise it's just my own fantasy.

Sarah Hall

BEES

ONE MORNING – not long after you've moved here – you're out in the garden of the house and you notice the ground is littered with insects. They lie here and there, dark between the tawny and honey southern pebbles, leggy and fossil-winged. It has become a garden of dead bees. You're close to the earth, attending to something on the ground, and now you can see the creatures strewn all about, petrified and bereft between the stones. Stiff, broken, geological things. Up close they are black-capped like aristocrats at a mass funeral, their antennae folded, mortuary-formal, across their eyes. Wearing bands of gold. Some of the bees have their back halves missing. Some are lying in two exact pieces. And some seem perfectly whole in their demise, as if having landed from flight in a timely fashion right at the end of their lifespan. This tiny London garden is a secret insect cemetery.

Since you arrived in the city you've been noticing details, in a tenderly open, empty way. You've been gathering them up, storing them. You're a hollow cistern with new information and experience trickling in. This is a new disposition for you – this vacancy. Always before you felt full, too full, and heavy with what had made you and who you were. You wonder if it's a prerequisite of living in such a metropolis, this scraping out of past existence from yourself to make way for a successive, enormously ornamented one. You've come down from the north where life seemed austere, minimal but turgid, and lit by a precise, slaughtering light. You've left the reticent moors, the mountains and rivers, the drench, the teal sky above the lakes. You've left the people who know you and have inured or injured you. It was not work-related, this move, not a promotion, an opportunity, that which beckons to the eager minds and ambitions of many rural dwellers. You've come away from your old home because of devastation or betrayal, a hot, vivid, personal tragedy, a reason you imagine to be prosaic here amid the vast molten cauldron of humanity. It is this – you've arrived under elegy, loss, grief of some kind. You've aimed your wound at London, assured that here above all places there must be a cure, an escape from the suffering. Or perhaps you just fled. But you've come to forget, to move on, to re-fill, to begin again. With this move here, some lurid internal part of you has unzipped your flesh and stepped outside. Something essential and red. You felt it go. You felt it split you open through the chest and gut, and tug through the dull walls of muscle and move off into the crowds. It happened the moment you arrived at Euston station. You're not sure what it was exactly that went, or how it relates to your condition, but it wrenched away, anguished and inflamed and angry and sick as it was. What's left now is a loose pink sack of human being, bearing your name and your forgettable history, a skin bag with a few grey organs and some blood slung in, which co-operate to the extent they must in order to keep you alive. With this move you've gouged yourself clean, made yourself airy inside, gentle and pastel. And you don't mind going without that prime red aspect of yourself. It has, for now, granted you some mercy.

The bees in the garden are strangely composed. They seem to have collected in groups, selected places together in which to expire, without rhyme or reason – there is a sinister quality to this but you don't register it. They seem jewel-like, obsidian and amber, set as they are into the shale. You bend and pick one up by a taut leg, place it in the palm of your hand and feel the dry bristle of it, like thorn and paper together. You're lucky to have the garden of course, desecrated insect population notwithstanding. You're lucky to be where you are now, lucky on a number of different levels. It could all have been very different. A bed-sit in Hackney, depositless and rank. A wrong doorbell rung, suitcase in hand, accompanied by the rationale that your one retaliatory indiscretion months ago may have left a residue of fondness, helpfulness, meaning. You've landed softly in one of the hardest of all cities, with only a few possessions weighing you down – just what you could carry in a suitcase – and a body freshly gutted of its redness and its past. You left where you lived because you had to, you'll keep reminding yourself of this whenever you need bracing or reassuring. An old friend made it possible, her flatmate moving out to be with a partner just when you needed a room. So you took it over, two months' rent up front. You didn't flinch over the price. There was no choice. She's another northerner, this friend, from the same soaked valley but one village over. You've kept in touch with her since school, sporadically or comprehensively, depending on each of your situations year in year out. She's never married. She's a professional and her dialect has now been rounded off, worn down by the south. She works in the publishing industry. You visited her a few times prior to moving, though it was hard getting away – you had to use Christmas shopping as an excuse – and you blew off steam down here, complained about the ignorance and pettiness and insulation of the borders, said you wished you'd left when you'd had the chance, too. Then you both shared fond memories of school and hill-walking when you were girls, and the old-men's pubs in your town, lost boyfriends. You filled her in on local gossip, what such-and-such was doing, who such-and-such was fucking. And then you cried, and, wordlessly, she comforted you. She knows a little about the circumstances of your moving here, only as much as you've conveyed. She'll not ask more, even though she must imagine it. She'll wait for you to broach the subject.

After the great fells, and the Pennines, the watery expanses and broad sweep of your home county, the garden here seems small, but is nice. There's a bench, being molested by untrimmed overgrown bushes, you think buddleia, you must ask your housemate at some point. A Mexican pot-bellied oven sits up at the top end by the kitchen window. There's a bird table. Plant pots. These things provided by your friend who has been here in the city for almost twelve years now, long enough to make it home, long enough to acquire possessions, a good circle of friends. She even has secateurs, trowels, packets of broom and violet seeds. She tends the garden to relax after work when she can but is endlessly tired from commuting and away much of the time. And you have the place to yourself, which is good in a way. You've been out here a few times, in this cultivated pocket of nature; mornings, to catch the sun as it breaks free of the rooftops – you're not yet working through the day. You've had glasses of wine in the evening with your housemate, she's keen to give you company when she can, and attention, in that familiar, unasking, concerned, dour, northern manner. It's then she tries to tell you it'll all be all right, her tone cursory, unassailable, but with more unspoken language underneath. You always nod, unconvinced. You've been out here at night when you can't sleep, the bed still feels too uncomfortable, foreign, or to cool down –

London's more humid than you imagined in the summer months. And you've also come out to investigate the frantic barking and rummaging going on around the bins and fences before sunrise – you've an ear for such things. You've been out to look at the yellow urban-stained moon. These are the moments you wonder why you've come to London, if it's right – these nocturnal, unquiet moments, when the north seems close, closer, connected as it always is by the moon. It's been difficult to reconcile the decision of course. It's been difficult to let go, and wholly forget, even though you have been cored of history, emotion. At night, in the dark frothy-edged garden, it occurs to you that it might even have been your heart that separated from you as you reached the capital. Leaving behind a circuit of confused blood, opaque with ingredients and silty with uncertainty. And an empty body, that mercifully feels nothing, and is a chamber waiting for a fresh content.

Perhaps this is why the details around you are compelling and necessary and flood in, to fill that void. You go into the city because it's a place you're supposed to go into, since you are now a resident. You encourage yourself to go out, busy yourself, turn your mind to new engagements. So you go to galleries and shopping districts. It's so different from the rural, the wet slates, barns, fields, your once-vernacular scenery. You've some money, and a cash-card that is still working for now. Soon you'll find employment, probably quite menial, you're not qualified highly, but for now you're acquainting yourself with London, distancing yourself from the time before. It is a faceted city, ornate, modern, the antithesis of everything you've known. But you aren't afraid of it. You just catalogue it. You've noted the reprising mechanics of the newer train station barriers which mirror the fashion in which you retrieve your underground ticket from the top-slot of the stile after processing – the slam of gates opening angrily if you snatch it back, a sleek breach if you're slower, and, when the stations are busy, a permissive openness ticket after ticket to allow the unstoppable herd through. You've observed the red lit X in the OXO building on the South Bank at dusk as the train passes by, and for no reason you've committed it to memory, given it storage space, a cerebral shelf, as if it were an inanimate trinket. You've memorised noises, chimes, traffic, electrical currents, the kinetic character of the place, colour codes, fixtures, fountains, statues. There are stale pavement smells, body odour smells, strong doorstep musk smells, green pond smells. City ducks sleep-folded in half on park waters like closed feathered books. Dogs are monitored for their filth, and if let loose they bowl fast into groups of stumpy pigeons, sending the birds scattering like grey skittles. There are underground winds, motion sensations, beeps, accents. Your head's begun to fill with such trivia, such minutiae. You're becoming an eccentric private collector of such banal irrelevant things. They've begun to line up along the mantel of your mind, haphazardly. The urban miscellanea. The civic clutter. Like keen junk. There is room for it all, carelessly placed and compiled, purposeless under the bloodless cortex of your brain. Space for it, now the past has gone. Now the red has gone.

But this curious natural oddity, this apocalypse of bees on your doorstep, is surprising and intriguing in a different way. You're interested in it. For the first time since you came south you find yourself aroused, engaged. Walking about in the garden, your eyes cast down, you wonder if a disease has seized the insects – the first indication of a plague travelling up the food chain, through wheat and udders to plates. You wonder if this is the beginning of a toxic overload that you've occasionally read about in science journals and magazines in the doctor's waiting room, farm leaflets. Or, if something has poisoned the pollen – pesticide, sewage, the ill blood of the city itself. There were those terrible rains shortly after you first came that swelled the Thames and the Victorian sewers past functional capacity, and bloated the fish and sent them up to the surface of the brown surge in white-bellied dull-silvered droves. Maybe this is a similar holocaust, in the air. You don't yet understand this location's terrain and natural calibration, its relationship with inhabiting creatures, not in the way you've always known how wild fell ponies graze on upland in summer and riverside in winter, and that sheep will remain hefted until struck off. Still, you notice lavender blooming tenaciously along wall tops and the cancerous lumps on the trunks of street trees and rats on the train tracks and flocks of birds strumming between telegraph-wire frets. In the garden you tread around the small dead beings carefully, agricultur-ally. There are more than ever strewn about, preserved by the summer heat, rotund and teasle-spiked. Coffin-crossed. Guil-lotined in half. Or immaculate. You pick up the frailest twig you can find, and thread it through the tight crooked tunnel of legs made by the bodies of three bees, beading them as if on to a necklace. Then you plant the twig upright in a crack between the paving stones under the lounge window, like a flag, or votive of some kind – why you do this you don't know. Looking over the garden fence, when you are sure your neigh-bours are absent, you can't quite focus well enough to see if their miniature boxed lawn is suffering from the same problem. You think not. This, then, could be an independent mystery. A macabre gift just for you.

You wonder where the thermal redness of you has disap-peared to. All that ire and agony and passion and hope that was furled up into a heated creature inside, making you angry and upset and wild for the last few years. Sometimes you think it can't have gone far, is roaming London, scorching and singeing the undergrowth as it moves. Sometimes you wonder if it has actually truly disappeared, faded, lost potency like any of life's traumas eventually do. Sometimes you imagine that when it broke out of you at the station it went back up north. Maybe it always belonged up there, even though you came away. Maybe it always knew where it would be most inflamed and brightest, where it belonged, and while you now operate as a pale collection vessel, it lives on in a fury back home, fiery with its own self. It could be back in the house that you shared together, you and he, the man you've left behind. If it was your abortive tortured heart that departed, that ruddy loving and loathing piece of you, it could be curled up in front of the coal stove right now next to his dog, or staring out of the front door at the Scar as the authentic heavy rain comes down, or bumping about in the passenger seat of the Land Rover, driving into town. And then you wonder about him too, of course, what he's doing. If he's managing. If he's thriving. If he's sorry. If he knows he might still own your busted burning-red heart, and that you're turning through this new life as dully and uselessly as a shed tractor tire.

The days pass by, nectar-warm, sticky summer city days. The garden remains littered with bees. You never see them dying. Not tumbling out of the sky, or slow-twitching on the ground, pedalling upside down, a frail wing vibrating into stillness. They are only ever corpses. All you ever see is their extinction, the inhabited autopsy table. You're always too late to catch a murder, a mass cult suicide, or witness the final realisation of the species that it should never have existed at all, should not have been granted the possibility of flight. It's not a bother to you, the carnage, you've been used to natural brutality, stillbirths, hunts, and those terrible pyres. But you want to know what's taking the bees, what's killing them. It's becoming a fascination. You go into the garden more frequently to investigate and you watch them while alive, twitching and scooping inside flower heads, and moving like loud over-burdened zeppelins in the air. There are plenty around. They seem ambivalent to the bodies underneath them. They seem able to thrive and continue on with their business, regardless, almost in the way bracken does on the fell slopes, growing right alongside and out of its last dead tide. When you are inside the house you pause at the bedroom window and squint out, wondering if the bees require privacy to pass on. You even consider going down to the library by the park to look up information about bee-keeping, just so you'll know more. The woman who farmed next to you up north also kept bees and sold jars of nectar but she never mentioned anything about strange extinctions, she never likened her hives to salmon end-grounds where whole batches die after fulfilling their duties to procreate, after travelling miles.

YOU OFTEN LOOK at your face in the bathroom mirror in the mornings. It's lined along the brow, around the eyes, at the corners of your mouth. It's the face of a person who has spent time outdoors, scowling around livestock, and has not been exposed to expensive cream and not anticipated romantic betterment, but has always made an effort and can use make-up. You're in your mid-thirties. You aren't old for this city, where youth stretches out into middle age, pushing it back further and further. You felt older in the countryside, comparatively. Old in your home town, where women of your age had children already sitting exams or getting pregnant themselves. You have no children. You might have had children, were at risk of having them young, staying, as you did, back from college when the others went off, and marrying before twenty. But you didn't want to have them, even though your husband did – imagining extra hands to help around the farm, or following the regular social path. Something stalled in you, resisted. It wasn't even him, wasn't a refusal set against his temper or his rustic dirt-nailed hands, his north-blue eyes that you know were cast over the bare rumps of other women, Saturday nights after the clubs shut. It was not pitted against his love. You just didn't feel that broody itch, that inclination. You never saw through a full conversation about it either, but always said you were busy, had to get on, and you avoided the topic. Even though you maintained a productive sex life, from the last year of school until that sore red ember began to glow in your chest. It defined you in the eyes of others early on, that association, the reputation for decent sex, it carried weight with your peers in the community. And it created a precedent maybe. You can remember the taste of him now, from years of practice, sour, salty. You can recall the smell of slurry and hay and diesel, the feel of him butting behind you, increasingly minimal in his inquiry, habitual in his climax. It wasn't hard being with him, staying with him, he used to be proud and prized, as you were too, a good match, a bonny pair from popular gender batches, and there was the mechanism of the territory that encouraged stasis and young marriage, though you can't blame that. He knew he'd take over the family business, you knew what the gap next to him constituted, and what it wouldn't fit.

You were bright, but reconciled. You didn't feel held back, you didn't always feel the urge to head for the city as you have done now. Not until he began to breach the contract in various ways. A slap to begin with, arguments consisting wholly of cuss words, an infection passed on through fluid, a rumour of illegitimate offspring, the gossip and dogma. And it lit you inside and smouldered your innards hotter and hotter like slut iron until the bloom got livid. And the disgrace and offence turned round and round behind your ribs, frenziedly, like a hurt mammal. And so your heart became a flaming animal. But you bore it, kept it in, even seeing those other women around, even being called frigid and useless, even the tenderness at the back of your throat from choking on him, forced to, the welts up inside, and under your eyes, even the possible three-year-old daughter, paid for informally, you found out. There were enormous work stresses, ravaging diseases that undid farmers, not mitigating but influential, and you often felt optionless. And you bore it. Until you couldn't bear it any more. You initiated a confrontation. And got one. You recovered, phoned your friend, and then you left. By then the thing in your chest was scratching to get out, and at the London terminal it finally clawed right through. He's not come down to find you, with shitty wellies and apologies or demands. Nor do you want him to. All that remains between you both is the historical red piece, missing somewhere now, that urgeful feral creation of a bad past, carrying flames along its back as it moves. You look at your face in the mirror. It was once a pretty northern face, perhaps it still is. You wonder if you'll ever be able to love again or use your body for more than this basic form of living. You know that the crimes of your old life cannot be any greater or lesser than those of the residents sprawling across the heaths and suburbs and districts on each side of your garden.

It is a garden of dead bees. And it's a mystery why. They line the ground, like ideas, some destroyed, some still intact. Then, one day, it isn't a mystery anymore. You're downstairs making tea. It's early, sunny again, warm, the end of summer. You haven't been outside yet today. You haven't looked in the bathroom mirror and thought about him or what's been lost from you and where it can be. From the window in the kitchen you can see outside and there in the corner of the shrubbery next to the wooden bench is a disruption of bright colour. So you look properly, give it your attention. You think you must be mistaken at first. But, no, you're not. It's a fox. It's true red, rust red, blaze red. It's big, though appears juvenile with over-sized ears, and it seems, more than anything else, oddly placed here, in the city, in this tiny plot. It's sitting upright, arch-jawed, snouty, and is scanning the scenery with eerie yellow eyes. You don't know if it can see you moving in the kitchen. You keep still and silent in case noise travels through the window glazing and out into the garden, disturbing the crea-ture, though there is as always the perpetual sound of the city to do that, the screech of trains, the acceleration of cars and the ordinary commotion of humans. Your housemate told you there were foxes in London, lots of them, urban scavengers responsible for tearing bin liners and scenting up lintels, but you didn't believe it, not really, not until now. You'll tell her she was right, when she gets home. You'll tell her everything. You feel oddly thrilled by this sighting, enlivened. The foxes you've seen up north seemed small, pale orange and discreet, sloping along roadsides at night, or cowering from the hounds, diminutive on the moors. This one is unapologetic, bold and striking, as if it owns this city allotment. It's captivating, fiery, like it's been stoked up from the surroundings to a high temperature. You watch it in your garden, a keen and covetous thing, its fur a furnace amid the undergrowth. And as you watch it, your heart starts up in earnest, raw, heated, a strong beat pushing the blood around. The fox tracks the resinous flight of an insect in the air nearby, eyes sparking like lit fuses. It opens its jaws then snaps them shut, un-stung and accurate, and shakes its head in a red fury.

Paul T. Owen

GUNFINGERS

HE KNEW SHE WOULD BE COMING IN as soon as he heard about the kid dying. He didn't know why she always came to him; he never knew much about it; this kind of thing was exactly the reason he'd split from the Jamaicans down the road. He didn't mind a bit of weed. But it was where that bit of weed got you when somebody else started selling weed where you were selling weed that he minded. And what you felt you had to do about it. He wanted to cut hair and he wanted to talk to the guys that came in and the girls they brought with them. The other stuff, he didn't want anything to do with it.

So he didn't know why she always came to him whenever anything big went off. Maybe she talked to a lot of people. Maybe she had no one else to talk to. He didn't mind, anyway. She was a nice woman, Anne-Marie, and he supposed it made him feel a bit important when she came around asking questions, and he liked it when he read something he'd told her quoted next to a false name in the paper the next week.

So he knew it wouldn't be long before she came in, and he was just buzzing the back of Jamal Stephens's head when she swung through the door. He put down the clippers and went over. 'Is Ricardo in?' she asked him.

'It's me,' he said. She never recognised him.

'Sorry,' she said, touching him apologetically on the shoulder. 'Sorry; that's so embarrassing.' They laughed.

'Do't worry,' he said. 'What's goin' on?'

'Yeah, not much, Ricardo. How are you?'

Donnie had stopped cutting at the chair next to him and was looking over.

'So how you keeping, Anne-Marie?' said Ricardo. Donnie turned his clippers back on and got on with trimming Lewis's hair.

'I'm fine,' she said. 'What about you? This place looks busy. Looks nice too.'

'Yeah,' he said. 'Thanks. I've been doing all right, so I thought, give the place a lick of paint, cheer everybody up, j'get me?'

'Are you still working hard?'

'I'm working hard, but that's OK. But I'm going away next week so I'll get a break.'

'Where are you going?'

'New York.'

'Nice. Be careful.'

'What, the war? I'll be all right. A black man ai't western. Mans won't touch me.'

'What are you going for?'

'You know Yolanda Harris, girl sings at the Headroom on Saturdays? Beautiful voice? You done a piece on her last year, I'm sure you did. I been managing her, you know, setting up spots for her to sing at, j'get me? She got a two-single deal with a record company, and we're going out there to film the video. They did make her change the name of one of her songs because of the whole – '

'September 11,' said Anne-Marie.

'September 11. That's right. "You're my Explosion" it was called. Just a love song, you know.'

'Well, brilliant, though,' said Anne-Marie. 'Where is she from, Yolanda? Is she from round here?'

'Stonebridge, she lives.'

'Well, listen, when are you going?'

'Next week.'

'I'll give you a ring before the end of the week and we'll do a piece on her, definitely. I'll send a photographer round to get a nice picture of her. That's great news.'

Jamal was still sitting there with his head half-shaved, starting to look a bit pissed off, so Ricardo switched on his clippers and took a couple of chunks of hair off to keep him quiet.

'Listen, you know why I've come to see you,' said Anne-Marie. 'The shooting.'

'Yeah,' he said. And then he said, 'I haven't got much to tell you, honestly.'

'Devon McColl. Did you know him?'

'I did't *know* him, but I knew him. If he came in here, I'd recognise him. He never came in here. But I'd seen him around.'

'Was he popular?'

'I do't know. I do't know if he was. He was just some young kid. There was no trouble either way that I knew of. He wasn't popular with guys I know. Not they were enemies. We just did't know the guy.'

'Was he just a traffic warden?'

'That's what people said. I never saw him do no traffic warden work but that's what people said he was, a traffic warden.'

'Was he a policeman?'

Ricardo shook his head. 'I never heard that. He was just a young kid, twenty, twenty-one. Too young for undercover, isn't it?'

'Listen,' she said. 'I know you're busy tonight. Somebody told me he drank in the Stag's Head and I want to talk to people in there, but I want to talk to them quietly and I want them to talk to me, and I can't really walk into the black half of that pub without everyone in there looking round at me and everyone in there will know exactly what I'm doing and no one'll talk to me.'

'You want me to come in with you?' he said.

'What time will you be finished here?' she said.

'We're not that busy, are we, Donnie? If I finish Jamal's hair now and then go down the road for half an hour you'll manage here all right, won't you?'

'Yeah, man. No problem,' said Donnie.

'We'll just wait in the car,' said Anne-Marie. 'You come and get us when you're finished.'

Ricardo knew she wouldn't be waiting in the car. She'd be out after another angle or talking to somebody else probably. He liked her because he felt like she was interested in what was happening here. She wasn't from Harlesden. She was from Scotland somewhere. But it rang true the way she wrote about Harlesden. She wrote good pieces. He knew a lot of guys who felt like when a guy was killed nobody should talk to the police, nobody should talk to the newspapers, although actually the more shootings there were, the less the papers seemed to come round, except for Anne-Marie. The bad boys thought it just needed dealing with themselves. But that way the next week Anne-Marie would be round asking questions about another brother.

Ricardo began to trace the shape of a ganja leaf on to the back of Jamal's head. He enjoyed it; it was inventive at least. A lot of cutting hair was conservative; it was about stopping growth, stopping change. All most people wanted when they came in was, 'Cut it so in three weeks' time it looks just like this again.'

HE STRODE DOWN the high street with Anne-Marie in tow.

'So listen,' Anne-Marie said. 'I'm going to go into the Irish side because I need to talk to the manager. Could you just go over the other side and have a look who's in there, and then ask a few guys to meet us round the side of the pub?'

'Sure, sure,' Ricardo said. He hated the Stag's Head. They called it the Apartheid Pub. When he'd first moved to Harlesden a guy had asked him to meet him in there, and he'd told Ricardo, 'Go in the first door. Do't go in the wrong door. One side is black people's side and the other side is for white people.' He'd thought, big deal. He'd been to plenty of places in Brixton where the white kids would sit at a few tables, say, around the pool table, and the black people would sit at some others, say, around the DJ booth. And the next night it would all change.

But when he had first walked into the Apartheid Pub he'd been shocked. The bar took up the middle of the room, splitting the pub into two. Each half had its own front door, and once you were inside there was no way to cross to the other section without going back outside and in again through the other door. In one half of the pub, blacks in their teens, twenties and thirties sat, drank, stood, smoked, joked and chatted each other up. In the other half were the Irish, middle-aged and older, sitting staring at the TV or muttering to each other through the sides of their mouths.

They walked past the Jamaican barbershop, his old workplace, his training ground, where two tall guys, Malik and Justin, leant on the sides of the door like sentries in Wu-Wear and white trainers. They didn't acknowledge Ricardo and he didn't acknowledge them. Outside the café where Devon McColl had been shot, Anne-Marie stopped to count the bullet-holes in the shutters and write down the messages on the cards on the bunches of flowers left there for the dead man. But they just said 'With love' and 'In peace' and that kind of thing, and Ricardo thought she wouldn't get many clues out of that. Kids walked past making gunfingers.

At the doors to the Stag's Head they separated, Ricardo walking in through the black entrance and Anne-Marie through the white one. As soon as Ricardo walked in his side he immediately saw two, three, four guys who he knew could help Anne-Marie. One of them he thought would definitely know something about the murder, but he would never talk to Anne-Marie about it so there was no point even asking him. Instead he went to the bar and thought about how to approach the others. Across the bar he saw Anne-Marie on her own side, talking to the manager beside a Guinness poster.

His rum and Coke arrived and he took it over to the wooden table where Ade and Ben sat with two men he didn't know, under a sign which read: 'Tables are for customers only. Those not buying drinks will be asked to leave.'

'Wha's happenin',' he said.

'Wha's goin' on,' Ade replied, and Ben took his hand with a clap.

'Good to see you, man, where you bin?' said Ben.

'Up the road. Always up the road,' Ricardo said. 'You think Ferguson's gonna get rid of Beckham?'

'Hope so,' said Ade.

'Forty million Real Madrid,' said Ben. 'Think he got the message when the man kicked that boot in his eye?' On the white side Anne-Marie was still talking to the landlord, and writing something down. They talked about Beckham for a while. When one of the guys he didn't know got up to go to the toilet and the other one got a call on his mobile, Ricardo said to Ade and Ben, 'Listen, man. There's a girl from the local paper wants to find out about that Devon McColl kid gettin' shot, j'get me? I do't know nothin' about it. She's a friend of mine, sort of. Will you come outside help me out?'

'What is she, the local paper?' said Ade.

'Yeah, blood. Anne-Marie Brown. She always writes about the shootings. She's all right, man.'

'I read a thing when that old geezer was stabbed,' Ben said.

'She do't need our names. Do't worry on that. She just do't want to come on to the black side. Will you come out and talk?'

'I do't know much, blood.'

'It's all right. Anything.'

He looked across at Anne-Marie as he stood up, and she said something to the landlord and then she left too. In the alleyway Ricardo introduced her.

'Did Devon drink in there often?' Anne-Marie asked them.

'Yeah, he did,' said Ade. 'But I did't really know him that well.'

Ben said, 'He was just a young kid, you know? He showed his face. You'd know him if he walked in.'

Ade said, 'I did't even know him, do't think.'

'Why do you think this happened?' said Anne-Marie.

'Could be . . . this, could be that,' said Ben. 'I ai't heard anything, really, y'know, have you, Ade?' said Ben.

'When he came in, who was he usually with? Did he ever seem to be arguing with anyone?'

'Nah, nah,' said Ade. 'Jus' a peaceful kid, j'get me?'

'And who was he usually with?'

'I do't know 'em, y'know. Do you know 'em, Ben?'

'I recognised one guy, but – '

'Do you know his name? Where he lives?'

'Nah, I do't . . . Do't think so.'

Soon the two men left. 'Sorry about that,' said Ricardo. 'They did't seem to know much, did they?'

'Do you know what Mick said? The landlord there?' said Anne-Marie. 'He told me that Devon used to drink in there. But he said he didn't know what went on over the other side; the black side, you know. He said he didn't want to. As long as they didn't fight in the pub – this is what he said – and didn't take drugs in the pub, whatever happened outside the pub was none of his business. He said that if a white man had been shot, all over the borough people would be going into the police stations to try and help catch whoever shot him, but I had no chance of finding anything out, because this kid was black. No one would come forward. He said.'

Ricardo looked at his watch. 'Do you know Johnny Thompson at the Proof Club? He might be setting up now if you want to have a word with him.'

'Good idea,' said Anne-Marie. And the two of them began to walk back up the street towards Proof.

Proof was the final building on the high street and it overlooked the low train tracks of Willesden Junction. If commuters came back late in the evening they could often see silhouettes moving, moving at the windows above their trains, and Proof was constantly getting into trouble over the volume of its music.

They knocked on the door, and after a minute or so a black man, aged around forty, opened up.

'Hello,' said Anne-Marie. 'Is Mr Thompson in?'

The man shook his head almost sadly. 'Nah, man. I've not seen him for three months.'

'Does he still run the place?' said Anne-Marie.

'He *runs* it, but I *run* it,' the man said.

'My name's Anne-Marie Brown. I'm a reporter for the local paper. I know Mr Thompson well.'

'Mm?' said the man, casting a wary eye over her and standing back from the door to usher them into the porch, where posters indicated prices and a cash box sat ready to receive the night's takings.

'Did you know Devon McColl?'

'Yeah, I knew him. I knew him well.'

'Was he a traffic warden?'

'Of course he was a traffic warden.'

'What was he doing down here that night?'

'I do't know. Drinking, maybe, or working. Perhaps he was giving out tickets.'

'Do you have any – you must have – do you have any theories about what happened to him? Why it happened?' she asked him.

'I think they got the wrong man,' he said. 'I think they got the wrong man. Devon was not into drugs or fighting or badness. He was a hard-workin' boy. *Legal* work. He didn't want to get mixed up in no badness. Not everybody out there is carrying a gun. I know brothers that are at university and college.'

'Of course, of course. Look, I'm not – so who – why would they think he was? Mixed up in it. Do you know?'

But then he wasn't looking at Anne-Marie any more, but over her shoulder, through the open door. 'Ah, I do't know. Listen – '

Ricardo turned to see a white man and a white woman walking from a neat, practical car towards the club door. They looked official and his first thought was that there was probably some kind of problem with the club's licence, but the two whites stopped at the doorway and pulled out police badges – very quickly; open and shut – and said, 'Hello, sorry to interrupt. Operation Trident. Can we come in?' And the club manager and the police officers melted away leaving Ricardo and Anne-Marie on the outside of the closed door.

'Trident down here,' said Anne-Marie. 'They mustn't have a fucking thing.'

WHEN HE WENT BACK to the barber's, Donnie was cleaning up. The pale lights from the mirrors lit up the white floor and the walls.

'What's goin' on, Donnie.'

'What's happening. You finish with that reporter girl?'

'Yeah.'

'You ought to be careful, blood, j'get me?'

'I saw the feds. Trident guys were down here.'

'They stopped me yesterday,' said Donnie. 'Saying did I see anything.'

'Did you see anything?'

'I was working like you, man.'

'Did you tell 'em that?'

'Yeah. They said they'd seen two hundred people on the CCTV that night and two people only had spoken to them. Thing is, why they *need* us to speak to them?'

'What d'you mean?' said Ricardo.

'Mans always talking about, we seen two hundred people on the CCTV, j'get me? Well, they got CCTV that can spot my car when I nip into the congestion charge and by the end of the week the bill is through my door, eighty quid. Why they not got CCTV that can spot the number plate when a car drive-by shoot someone, j'get me?'

'I don' know. All Ken's cameras are brand-new, isn't it? In the congestion charge zone. Brand-new cameras. Here it's all old cameras.'

Ricardo put down his broom. 'You tell me that if Prince Charles was to drive through Harlesden and a shot rang out mans wouldn't have the number plate by 10 a.m. the next day,' he said.

'But look,' said Ricardo. 'But look. This isn't – this isn't – look, you can say white man do't put no high priority on us. You can say that. But this ai't – it ai't no white man killing us here, j'get me? It's us killing each other. And no one's speaking out try and stop it.'

'Fuck speak out. Because if you come forward, they think, police think: He knows something about this, he must be mixed up in guns, j'get me, and if he ai't mixed up in guns, he's mixed up in drugs, and if he ai't mixed up in drugs, he's gotta be mixed up in something, and when they can't find the shooter and they feel like a bunch of pussies mans bring you back in again because at least they can get you, one more bad man, one more criminal off the streets, what they say, and you're fucked, isn't it.'

'Do you know who killed him?'

'I do't know who killed him, but I know mans that would know, or I know mans that know mans who know. But I ai't about to arks them.'

'Why?'

'Because I'm keeping my head down, j'get me?' said Donnie. 'I'm keeping out of it. Because I do't want to be next. Mans talking 'bout everybody knows who killed him, but feds won't touch him – they won't touch who did it – because they prob'ly already know him as a known informer. So they ai't gonna do shit to him. And listen, man, what I talk to them –

what if there's shit I know that only I know, j'get me? What if that shit gets out and this brother knows I told it? No no no. And police talk about you give evidence they'll protect you. I do't wanna be protected. I do't wanna a new life, new name. I'm happy right here,' and he stamped the broom down like a foot.

Everything was nearly finished for the night, and Donnie took off. Ricardo locked up the shop and pulled the shutters down, and walked up the road to his flat. Three red dots marked out a plane in the blue-black sky above. He locked the door, and then drew the bolt, and then flipped the other key, and then he sank into his comfortable sofa. He didn't feel angry. He felt lucky.

Devon McColl was twenty, twenty-one. How old was Laurence now? He must have been seventeen or eighteen, Ricardo reckoned. He flipped the TV on to Channel 4, and a burst of gunfire filled the flat. He turned the volume down. On the screen, an American cop fell back through a rooftop window into a grimy bedroom, returning fire as he landed. He thought he should really go and see Laurence, find out what he was up to nowadays. The kid had rung him the other day; a few days ago now, couple of weeks, maybe, asked him something about the DLR. He should ring him back, make sure he was doing all right.

HE SAW in the paper that the funeral was that Thursday, and on Thursday he asked Donnie to hold the fort while he went out to buy some supplies for the shop, and then he nipped home and changed into his black suit, and walked over the railway bridge towards the church. There was a stillness in the air and he could hear birds singing in the cemetery.

He slipped in at the back. It was crowded. Women in black shawls and wide-brimmed hats kissed each other on the cheek and young men muttered to one another in clumps. Ricardo tried not to meet anyone's eye. An old lady shuffling past him gave his shoulder a squeeze, probably thinking he was gazing at the floor in sorrow. More and more people paced past him until all the seats were full, and still they came, standing along the sides of the church and in the doorways.

He stood to let an elderly lady sit in his place, and tried to blend into the back wall. Near the front, a middle-aged woman bit her lip as she took in the size of the congregation with her eyes, and he saw her hand tighten on another lady's arm. The tall, grey-haired reverend appeared, stooped and bent with age, and approached her, clutching both her arms up high, almost at the shoulder. Ricardo was passed a hymn sheet adorned with a picture of the smiling, cheeky face of Devon McColl. He looked very young.

Eventually the service began, and gospel hymns flooded into the crowd. Ricardo, who had no idea he still remembered any of these songs, found himself swept along as the congregation sang. He spotted Anne-Marie near the front of the church and leant back next to a curtain so she wouldn't see him.

The reverend told them Devon's sister would speak next. A pretty girl of eleven or twelve began to climb up from the pews. Just as she had almost got to her feet, her mum grabbed her arm and pulled her back, kissing her on the cheek and holding her tight. Both of them were crying.

'When you were kind, we saw it,' she said. 'We felt it. Don't worry 'bout that, Devon. We always saw it.' She breathed hard, catching her breath.

'Oh Lord, look at her,' whispered a woman beside Ricardo.

'I can't believe somebody took you away,' said the girl. 'Devon was a lovely – lovely brother, and I'll always miss him so much.' She sniffed. 'I wanted to sing him – it was his favourite hymn. He used to like to sing it at church when he was little.' And she began to sing. Ricardo realised he knew this one too: 'I am Free'. 'Praise the Lord, I'm free,' the little girl sang, unaccompanied, 'no longer bound, no more chains holding me,' but she couldn't carry on, and after one more line rushed back into the embrace of her mother, and the reverend stood up again.

When Devon's father spoke, the air in the church became heavy suddenly. Ricardo watched as people sat forward to catch his words. He got up from the row behind Devon's mother, and didn't look at her, and Ricardo suddenly knew – knew for sure, although he couldn't say how – that they must have broken up somewhere along the way, that this death must have broken them up. The father started falteringly, reading from a piece of A4 paper, but as he spoke he scanned the eyes of the congregation and the paper stayed limp in his hand.

'When I was young and I came to this country I thought it was another world. I thought it was a wonderful place. I thought, "Here my children can have everything they want,"' he said. 'It wasn't like that. I know now it's not like that. I was worried, when you read about the shootings, when you see the kids running and hear the police sirens in the night. You worry about where your boy is. And you tell yourself it's stupid. You're being silly. He'll be fine. And then one night he wasn't fine.

'Devon never hurt anybody. Even if he was mixed up in drugs, or guns, or stealing, or badness, it would not make it right, what happened. But he wasn't. He wasn't, and everybody here knows he wasn't. He was a good boy. He was a good boy to his mother and his little sisters and he was a good boy to me. He was a bright boy. Everybody here knows that.

'And I don't know why this happened. I don't know why anybody would – *shoot* and *kill* my boy. That's what happened. It wasn't *noble*. It wasn't *tragic*. It was horrible. It was a mess. No one there to wipe his sweat. And next time you hear those sirens go past, you have to think: it isn't TV. It isn't a game. Something's going on here that's not good. Tonight somebody – a real living boy – has been hurt and somebody's mother is going to have to hold him when he comes home crying, if he comes home at all. And I want you to stop and think now, I want you all to stop and really think hard, and if anybody wants to come and tell me anything here today, anything at all in confidence, I want to hear it. I really want to hear it. I want to know what happened. I want to know why it happened.'

He coughed, and looked again at his notes. 'I know that when they find the man who did this,' he said. 'I will have to find it in me, in myself to forgive him. I'll have to find it some-where. It's in there. It's got to be in there. I just can't see it right now.' There were sympathetic smiles from the mourners. 'But I'll do it. Because if we don't do it, this goes on and on, on and on until somebody else's boy is lying here – ' He flung his hand in the direction of the casket. 'I know what it means. It means a father speaking out against his son, or a mother, or a sister or a brother or a friend. But the truth sometimes hurts. The truth sometimes does hurt. We've got to be our brother's keeper. Come and talk to me. Come and talk to me.' And he sat down.

Ricardo stayed where he was until the church had almost completely emptied out, and then caught the edge of the mourning procession as it trudged its way to the cemetery, avoiding the cars trolling slowly into and out of the cemetery gates, and down the narrow, dusty pathways that led relatives to their loved ones, buried among the dead grass. He was struck again by the beauty and elegance of some of the older graves, really old he meant, graves from the last century adorned with tiny statues of Mary and Jesus, arms broken off now on many of them, heads broken off, some opening welcoming hands as they greeted the humble spirits at the gates of Heaven. The mourners kept their eyes on the ground.

He thought of Laurence, who was not much younger than Devon. Where did Laurence spend his nights? Ricardo admitted that he didn't know. He didn't really know who Laurence was any more. He'd be all right; he was a quiet boy, he thought, but then he thought: Was he? Was he still? At Christmas Laurence had slipped out after dinner while they were all watching TV, and awoken Ricardo, who'd been sleeping on the sofa, when he rolled in at 3 a.m. Where had he been? Ricardo hadn't asked him, just turned over and pulled the cover over his head as his brother crossed the lounge to the bathroom. Ahead, the route curved, and the heavy brown coffin swung into view on the heaving shoulders of the six pall-bearers, following in the footsteps of the aged, bent old reverend. He watched Devon's father take the weight of his boy at the front of the coffin with an intake of breath, and felt a pang of anger suddenly for his own father, who had left his wife, his sons and his daughter when Ricardo was about fifteen. God knew, it was his own business who his dad set up home with, but did it have to mean cutting out his old family altogether? He never saw Ricardo's mum, never saw Laurence, never saw Marissa. Ricardo only saw him when he went out of the way to make the effort, and even then his father often called to cancel in the hours before they were due to meet. And hardly asked about Laurence or Marissa. Ricardo ended up pretending to his brother and sister his dad had talked about them, and giving them money out of his own pocket that he told them was his dad's.

But the pang didn't go away, and he realised suddenly as they lowered the coffin that it was not anger, it was guilt. Since he'd set up out here in Harlesden he'd hardly looked back. And he realised for the first time that when he looked at Laurence he saw his dad's eyes and when he heard the bitterness that had begun creeping into Laurence's voice that Christmas he knew exactly where that bitterness came from. And he hated that bitterness and he hated those eyes. He swallowed and watched the earth fall. He would make sure to call Laurence when he got in that night. More than that. He would make sure to go and see him.

Hanif Kureishi

LONG AGO YESTERDAY

FEELING LOST ONE EVENING just after my fiftieth birthday, I pushed against the door of a pub not far from my childhood home. My father, on the way back from his office in London, was inside, standing at the bar. Dad didn't recognise me but I was delighted, almost ecstatic, to see the old man again, particularly as he'd been dead for ten years, and my mother for five.

'Good evening,' I said, standing next to him. 'Nice to see you.'

'Good evening,' he replied.

'This place never changes,' I said.

'We like it this way.'

I ordered a drink; I needed one.

I noticed the date on a discarded newspaper and calculated that Dad was just a little older than me, nearly fifty-one. For the first time we were as close to equals – or at least contemporaries – as we'd ever be.

He was talking to a man sitting on a stool next to him, and the barmaid was laughing extravagantly with them both. Dad looked at me without recognition but I knew him better than anyone, or thought I did, and I was inclined to embrace him or at least kiss his hands, as I used to. I refrained but watched him looking comfortable at the bar beside the man I now realised was the father of a schoolfriend. Neither of them minded when I joined in.

Like a lot of people, some of my best friendships are with the dead. I dreamed frequently about both my parents and the house, undistinguished though it was. Of course I'd never imagined Dad and I might meet up like this, for a conversation.

Lately I have been feeling unusually foreign to myself. My fiftieth hit me like a tragedy, with a sense of wasted purpose and many wrong moves made. I can hardly complain: I am a theatre and film producer, with houses in London, New York and Brazil. But complain I will. I have become keenly aware of various mental problems which enervate but do not devastate me.

I ran into Dad on Monday. The previous weekend I'd been staying with some friends in the country who have a fine house and pretty acquaintances, paintings you want to look at, and an excellent cook. The Iraq war, which had just started, had been on TV continuously. About twenty of us, old and young men, lay on deep sofas drinking champagne and giggling: but the prospect of thousands of bombs smashing into donkey carts, human flesh and primitive shacks, had depressed everyone in the house. We were aware that disgust was general in the country and that Blair, once our hope after years in opposition, was already the most tarnished, cheap, and loathed leader since Anthony Eden. We were living through a time of lies, deceit and alienation. This was heavy, and our lives seemed light and uncomfortably trivial in comparison.

Today, after lunch, when I had left my friend's house – the taxi had got me as far as the station – I realised I'd left behind a bent paperclip I'd been fiddling with. It was in my friend's library where I'd been reading about mesmerism in the work of Maupassant, as well as Dickens's experiments with hypnotism, which got him into a lot of trouble with the wife of a friend. I hurried into the room to retrieve the paperclip, but the cleaner had just gone. Did I want to examine the contents of the vacuum cleaner?

My hosts were making faces at one another. Yet I was beginning to see myself as heroic in terms of what I achieved in spite of my obsessions. This was a line my therapist used. Luckily I would be seeing the good doctor the next day, before going to the theatre studio I had just set up.

Despite my devastation over the paperclip, I returned to the station and got on the train. I had come down by car; it was only now I realised that the route of the train meant we would stop at the suburban railway station nearest to my childhood home. As we drew into the platform I found myself straining to see things I recognised, even familiar faces, though I had left the area some thirty years before. But it was raining hard and almost impossible to make anything out. Then, when we were about to pull away, I grabbed my bag and stepped off the train, walking out into the street with no idea what I would do.

Near the station there had been a small record shop, a bookshop and a place to buy jeans, along with several pubs which I'd been taken to as a young man by a local bed-sit aesthete, the first person I came out to. [Of course he knew straight away.] His hero or model was Jean Cocteau. We'd discuss French literature and Wilde and Pop, before taking our speed pills and applying our make-up in the station toilet, and getting the train into the city. Along with another [white] friend who dressed as Jimi Hendrix, we saw all the plays and shows. Eventually I got a job in a West End box-office. This led to work as a stage hand, usher, dresser – even a director – before I found my 'vocation' as a producer of plays and films.

Now I asked my father his name and what he did. I knew how to work Dad, of course. Soon he was more interested in me than in the other man. Yet my anxiety didn't diminish: didn't we look similar? I wasn't sure. My clothes, as well as my sparkly new teeth, were more expensive than his, and I am heavier and taller, about a third bigger all over – I have always worked out. But my hair is going grey: I don't dye it. Dad's hair was still mostly black.

An accountant all his life, my father had worked in the same office for fifteen years. Soon he was telling me that he had two sons: Dennis, in the Air Force, and me – Billy. A few months ago I'd gone away to university, where, apparently, I was doing well. My all-female production of 'Waiting for Godot' – 'a bloody depressing play', according to Dad – had been admired. I wanted to say, 'But I didn't direct it, Dad, I only produced it. That has always been my problem.'

I had introduced myself to Dad as Peter, the name I some-times adopted, along with quite a developed alternative char-acter, during anonymous sexual encounters. Not that I needed a persona: Father would begin to ask me about myself, where I was from, what I did, but whenever I began to answer he would interrupt with a stream of advice and opinions.

My father said he wanted to sit down because his sciatica was playing up, and I joined him at a table. Regarding the barmaid, Dad said, 'She's lovely, isn't she?'

'Lovely hair,' I said. 'Unfortunately none of her clothes fit.'

'Who's interested in her clothes?'

This was an aspect of Father I'd never seen; perhaps it was a new departure for him. I'd never known him to go to the pub after work; he came straight home. Having secured Father for myself once Dennis had left – I had had to be patient, but knew always that the day would come – I'd be waiting for my father at the bus stop, ready to take his briefcase. In the house I'd make him a cup of tea while he changed.

Now the barmaid came to our table to remove the glasses and empty the ashtrays. She leaned across the table. Dad put his hand behind her knee and slid it all the way up her skirt to her arse, which he caressed, squeezed and held until she reeled away and stared at him in disbelief, shouting that she hated the pub and the men in it, and would he get out before she called the landlord and he flung him out personally?

'Out, out, out!' she reiterated. The landlord did indeed rush over. He snatched away Dad's glass, raising his fist.

Father got up and hurried to the door, flinching from a blow to his back, forgetting his briefcase. I'd never known Dad go to work without his briefcase, and I'd never known him leave it anywhere. As my brother and I would say, his attaché case was always attached to him. In homage, since university, I always carried a briefcase containing my glasses, newspaper, notebooks, novels, manuscripts.

Outside, where Dad was brushing himself down, I handed him his bag.

'Thank you.' I was walking with him. 'Shouldn't have done that,' he said. 'But once, just once, I had to. Suppose it's the last time I touch anyone!' He asked, 'Which way are you going?'

'I'll walk with you a bit,' I said. 'My bag isn't heavy. I'm passing through. I work in the office of a theatrical producer. I need to get a train into London but there's no hurry. I like being in odd places, not knowing where I am.'

He said, 'Why don't you come and have a drink at my house?'

My parents lived according to a strict regime, mathematical in its exactitude. Why, now, was he inviting a stranger to his house? I had always been his only friend; our passionate love kept us both busy.

'Are you sure?'

'Yes,' he said. 'Come.'

Noise and night and water streaming everywhere: you couldn't see further than your hand. We both knew the way,

Dad moving slowly, his mouth hanging open to catch more air. He seemed happy enough, perhaps with what he'd done in the pub, or maybe my company cheered him up.

Yet when we turned the corner into the familiar road, I felt absorbed in coldness until I was shivering. In my recent dreams – fading as they were like frescos in the light – the street was darkly dismal under yellow light, and over-abundant with white flowers and a suffocating, deathly odour, like being buried in roses. But how could I falter now? Once inside the house Dad threw open the door to the living room. I blinked; there she was, Mother knitting in her huge chair with her feet up, an open box of chocolates on the small table beside her, her fingers rustling for treasure in the crinkly paper.

Dad left me while he changed into his pyjamas and dressing gown. The fact he had a visitor, a stranger, didn't deter him from his routine, outside of which there were no maps.

I stood in my usual position just behind Mother's chair. Here, where I didn't impede her enjoyment with noise, complaints or the sight of my face, I explained that Dad and I had met in the pub, and he'd invited me back for a drink.

Mother said, 'I don't think we've got any drink, unless there's something left over from last Christmas. Drink doesn't go bad, does it?'

'It doesn't go bad.'

'Now shut up,' she said. 'I'm watching this. D'you watch the soaps?'

'Not much.'

Maybe the ominous whiteness of my dreams had been stimulated by the whiteness of the things Mother had been knitting and crocheting – headrests, gloves, cushion covers: there wasn't a piece of furniture in the house without a knitted thing on it. To this day I couldn't buy a pair of gloves without thinking I should only be wearing Mother's.

In the kitchen I made a cup of tea for myself and Dad. Mum had left my father's dinner in the oven: sausages, mash and peas, all dry as lime by now, and placed on a large cracked plate, with space between each item. Mum had asked me if I wanted anything but how would I have been able to eat anything here?

Waiting for the kettle to boil, I washed up the familiar dishes; I stood in the same position at the sink overlooking the garden. Then I carried Father's tea and dinner into his study, formerly the family dining room. With one hand I had to make a gap for the plate at the table, which was piled high with the books I would fetch for him from the local library.

Before, when I finished my homework, Dad liked me to go through the radio schedules, marking up programmes I might record for him. If I was lucky, he would read to me, or talk about the lives of the artists he was absorbed with – these were his companions. Their lives were exemplary but only a fool would try to emulate them. Meanwhile I would slip my hand inside his pyjamas and tickle his back, scratch his head or rub his arms until his eyes might roll a little in appreciation.

Now in his bedwear, and coming in and sitting down to eat, Dad told me he was embarked on a 'five-year reading plan'. He was working on *War and Peace*. Next it would be *The Remembrance of Things Past*, then *Middlemarch*, all of Dickens, Homer, Chaucer and so on. He kept a separate note-book for each author he read.

'This methodical way,' he pointed out, 'you will get to know everything in literature. You will never run out of interest, of course, because then there is music, painting, in fact the whole of human history – '

His talk made me recall winning the school essay prize for a tract on time-wasting. It was not about how to fritter away one's time profitlessly, which might have made it a useful and lively work, but about what can be achieved by filling every moment with activity! Dad was my ideal. He would read even in the bath, and as he reclined there my job was to wash his feet, back and hair with soap and a flannel. When he was done I'd be waiting with a warm, open towel.

I interrupted him, 'You certainly wanted to know that woman this evening.'

'What? How quiet it is! Shall we hear some music?'

He was right. Neither the city nor the country were quiet like the suburbs, the silence of people holding their breath.

Right away Dad was holding up a record he had borrowed from the library. 'You will know this but not well enough, I will guarantee.'

Beethoven's Fifth was an odd choice of background music, but how could I sneer? Without such enthusiasm my life would never have been full of music. Mother had been a church pianist and she took us to the ballet, usually *The Nutcracker*, or to see the Bolshoi when they visited London. Mum and Dad would go ballroom dancing; I loved it when they dressed up. Out of such minute inspirations I have found meaning sufficient for a life.

Dad said, 'Do you think I'll be able to go in that pub again?'

'If you apologise.'

'Better leave it a few weeks. I don't know what overcame me. That woman's not a jewess is she?

'I don't know.'

'Usually she's happy to hear about my aches and pains, and who else is, at our age?'

'Where d'you ache?'

'It's the walk to and from the station, sometimes I just can't make it, I have to stop and lean against something.'

I said, 'I've been learning massage.'

'Ah.' He put his feet in my lap. I squeezed his feet, ankles and calves; he wasn't looking at me now. He said, 'Your hands are strong. You're not a plumber, are you?'

'I've told you what I do. I have the theatre, and now I'm helping to set up a teaching foundation, a studio for the young.'

He whispered, 'Are you homosexual?'

'I am, yes. Never seen a cock I didn't like. You?'

'Queer? It would have shown up by now, wouldn't it?' He murmured, 'I've never done much about it.'

'You've never been unfaithful?'

'I've always liked women.'

'Do they like you?'

'The local secretaries are friendly. Not that you can do anything. I can't afford a "professional".'

'How often do you go to the pub?'

'I've started popping in after work. My Billy has gone.'

'For good?'

'After university he'll come running back to me, I can assure you of that. Around this time of night I'd always be talking to him. There's a lot you can put in a kid, without them knowing it. My wife doesn't have a word to say to me. She doesn't like to do anything for me, either.'

'Sexually?'

'She might look large to you, but in the flesh she is even larger, and she crushes me like a gnat in bed. I can say we haven't had it off for eighteen years.'

'Since Billy was born?'

He said, letting me caress him, 'She never had much enthusiasm for it. Now she is indifferent . . . frozen . . . almost dead.'

I said, 'People are more scared of their own passion than they are of anything else. But it's a grim deprivation she's made you endure.'

He nodded. 'You dirty homos have a good time, I bet, looking at one another in toilets and that . . .'

'People like to think so. I've lived alone for five years.'

He said, 'I am hoping she will die before me, then I might have a chance . . . We ordinary types carry on with these hateful things only for the single reason of the children and you'll never have that.'

'You are right.'

He indicated photographs of me and my brother. 'Without those babies there is nothing for me. It is ridiculous to try to live for yourself alone.'

'Don't I know it? Unless one can find others to live for.'

'I hope you do!' he said. 'But it can never be the same as your own.'

If love might interfere with the mortification of fidelity, there are always the children. I had been Dad's girl, his servant, his worshipper; my belief kept him alive. It was a 'cult of personality' he had set up; my brother and I were his mirrors.

Now Mother opened the door – not so wide that she could see us, or us her – and announced she was going to bed.

'Goodnight,' I called.

Dad was right about the kids. But what could I do about it? I had bought an old factory and at my own expense had converted it into a theatre studio, a place where young people could work with established artists. I spent so much time in this building that I had moved my office in. It would be where I would go when I left here, sitting in the café, seeing who would turn up and what they wanted from me, gradually divesting myself, as I aged, of all I'd accumulated. One of father's favourite works was Tolstoy's 'How Much Land Does a Man Need?'

I said, 'With or without children you are still a man. There will be things you want that children cannot provide.'

He said, 'We all, in this street, are devoted to hobbies.'

'The women too?'

'They sew or whatever. There's never an idle moment. My son has written a beautiful essay on the use of time.'

He sipped his tea; the Beethoven, which was on repeat, boomed away. He seemed content to let me work on his legs. As he didn't want me to stop, I asked him to lie on the floor. With characteristic eagerness he removed his dressing gown and then his pyjama top; I massaged every part of him, calling 'Dad, Dad,' under my breath. When at last he stood up I was ready with his warm dressing-gown, which I'd placed near the radiator.

It was late but not too late to leave. It was never too late to leave the suburbs but Dad invited me to stay. I agreed; it hadn't occurred to me that he would suggest I sleep in my old room, in my bed.

He accompanied me upstairs and in I went, stepping over record sleeves, magazines, clothes, books. My piano I was most glad to see. I can still play a little but my passion was writing the songs which were scrawled in notebooks on top of the piano. Not that I would be able to look at them. When I began to work in the theatre I didn't show my songs to anyone and eventually came to believe they were a waste of time.

Standing there petrified by the cold, I had to tell myself the truth and admit that my secret wasn't that I hadn't propagated, but that I'd wanted to be an artist. If I chose, I could blame my parents: they had seen themselves as enthusiastic spectators, in the background of life. But it was me who'd lacked the nerve – to fail, to succeed, to engage with the whole undignified, insane attempt at originality. I had only ever been a handmaiden, first to Dad and then to others – all the artists I'd supported – and how could I have thought it would be sufficient?

My bed was narrow. Through the thin ceiling I could hear my father snoring already; I knew when he turned over in bed. It was true that I had never heard them making love. Somehow, between them, they had converted the notion of physical love into a ridiculous idea. Why would anyone want to do anything so awkward with their limbs?

I couldn't hear Mother. She didn't snore but she could sigh for England. I got up and went to the top of the stairs. By the kitchen light I could see her in her dressing-gown, stockings around her ankles, trudging along the hall and into each room, wringing her hands as she went, muttering back to the ghosts clamouring within her skull.

She stood still to scratch and tear at her exploded arms. During the day she kept them covered because of her 'eczema'. Now I watched while flakes of skin fell on to the carpet, as though she were converting herself into dust, and she dispersed the shreds of her body with her dancer's delicately pointed foot.

As a child – even as a young man – I would no more approach Mother in this state than I would an exploded bomb. She had always made it clear that the uproar and demands of two boys were too much for her. Naturally, she couldn't wish for us to die so she died herself, inside.

One time my therapist asked whether Dad and I were able to be silent together. More relevantly, I should have said, was whether Mother and I could do this without me chattering on about whatever occurred to me, in order to distract her from herself. Now I made up my mind and walked down the stairs, watching her all the while. She was like difficult music and you wouldn't want to stand too close. But as with such music I'd advise anyone to forget trying to make it out but rather to sit with it, waiting for it to address you.

I was standing beside her and with her head down she looked at me with sideways eyes.

'I'll make you some tea,' I said and she even nodded.

Before, during one of her late-night wanderings, she had found me masturbating in front of some late-night TV programme. It must have been some boy group, or Bowie, I hope. 'I know what you are,' she had said. She was not disapproving, either. She was just a lost ally.

I made a cup of lemon tea and took it to her. As she stood sipping it I took up a position beside her, my head bent also, attempting to see – as she appeared to vibrate with inner electricity – what she saw and felt. It was clear there was no chance of me ever being able to cure her. I could only have been less afraid of her madness. Getting out had been the only option.

In his bed Father was still snoring. He wouldn't have liked me to be with her. Father had taken her sons for himself, charmed them away, and he wasn't a sharer.

She was almost through with the tea and getting impatient. Wandering, muttering, scratching: she had important work to do and time was passing. I couldn't detain her any more.

I slept in her chair in the front room.

When I got up my parents were having breakfast. My father was back in his suit and Mother in the uniform she wore to work in the supermarket. I dressed rapidly in order to join Dad as he walked to the station. It had stopped raining.

I asked him about his day but couldn't stop thinking about mine. I was living, as my therapist enjoyed reminding me, under the aegis of the clock. I wanted to go to the studio and talk; I wanted to eat well and make love well, go to a show and then dance, and make love again. I could not be the same as them.

At the station in London we parted. I said I'd always look out for him when I was in the area.

Louise Hocking

SCRATCH THE SURFACE

WE LOOKED LIKE THE EPITOME of London cool. Plumper than Kate M, as kooky as that Tara P-T, as mainstream with outsider appeal as Madness. We could only live in London. Camden to be specific.

We went off to Downing Street in 1997 to cheer Tony, and suffered the next day at work. Suffered ever since, some might say. Outwardly we had good jobs, a moral conscience, a trendy but quirkily beautiful flat. A cat who enjoyed a balcony but no garden and in true Blitz spirit still managed to catch a pigeon. Envied by my northern college friends, facing embitterment from my suburban relatives, we had it made.

Some might say that Camden was past its best. The council never got it back after the strike and it quickly lost its lead in the HIV pioneering health superiority. The market became a touted tourist attraction and the Body Shop became a shop rather than a stall. You couldn't feign a pseudo-persona as a fake photographer and take photos of weird and wonderful people any more. The café with rabbits in the garden had been replaced by what, well, just a café really. You were limited in getting a veggie breakfast at a restaurant where the most recently recruited waitress might go on to become a famous TV star in a Dennis Potter drama.

However, those of us in the know (for this please read me and mine), we still knew how to live it well. Our lives were a carefully crafted set of framed black-and-white stills. Each still glamorous and enviable. Any still of our life could be on your poly students' wall. If polys still existed.

On the nights we weren't enjoying close-up music at the Jazz Café, we were drinking fatty-latte at the Tate, promiscuously favouring the Modern, then the Britain, and then the Modern again. We went home and ate fish and chips, plantain and bacon, falafel and pitta bread, salt fish and akee, shepherd's pie, calalloo soup. The epitome of cosmopolitan life.

It's Saturday, any Saturday, any week, any month.

What's this? As we are shopping in Camden Sainsbury's, soon after the glass-in-baby-food scare, one of us looks a little down. Get closer. One of us looks downtrodden. Her eyes are dead and glassy, looking nowhere and seeing nothing. Clothes by Nicole Farhi, groceries by Waitrose, life by fear.

When we get home, one of us looks for every small sign to read the mood of the other. Pays for alcohol on an over-used credit card to avoid a row, safe in the knowledge that the row will only escalate, fuelled by the drinking. Strange logic maybe, but logic applies only in another life.

His friends call round. Everyone drinks, has fun. Except her. She can't risk it. She goes and lies on the bed, leaving them having their party. She listens to the Jubilee line nearby and thinks of throwing herself under it. He comes up and asks her why she is spoiling the fun, why is she putting a downer on everything, why is she ruining the party, what's wrong with her. She refreshes her make-up and comes downstairs. He still looks annoyed; she behaves anxiously. Prim and judgemental. He drinks more.

He's had enough.

Of her.

And her patronising ways.

Always making him feel bad about himself.

He gets up and grabs her by the scruff of the neck. Her hair is long and thick, easy to get a good grip. The room stands still. His male friends know instinctively this is a man-and-woman thing and maybe necessary. His female friends find her a bit off-hand anyway, and feel less than compassionate. They don't know what she's been up to. She might even deserve it.

She was always a bit aloof.

As he is hustling her out of the room, he starts to kick her on the legs and lower body. He needs to twist her hair hard, to contort her body to access her thighs and abdomen for kicking as these two actions are difficult for him to coordinate. He kicks and drags her up the stairs, back to her earlier place of refuge and suicide planning. Her legs are scrambling as someone running up a sand dune. She looks uncoordinated and stupid, just adding to the shame and humiliation. No one comes to help. Their lack of outrage adds to the belief in her mind that it might just all be true. It really is all her fault.

They reach the bedroom in a scrappy heap. He holds her by the neck against the wall and abuses her with every word that might make her despise herself. He needn't bother. She is there already. Maybe it helps him.

His thumb and forefinger span her constricted throat, touching her earrings. They are beautiful and he chose them especially for her last birthday. She tries to swallow but realises she can't. Not to worry, it seems the least of her problems. His hoarse voice leers obscenities. He is very close and she can feel bitter brandy-soaked spittle flecking her cheeks. They are only usually this close for love-making. In her extreme fear she focuses on some random detail to remove herself from her reality. She notices his teeth are dirty and she is somewhere else. She is at a tai chi class, she is on the South Bank watching lovers canoodle, she is welcoming everyone to her new book club, she is doing a jaunty mambo step at Bar Salsa.

He raises his right hand, holding her high against the wall with his left. It is too high, she looks like she is being prepared for some beautiful African jewellery to fit comfortably in with a Masai tribe. Band upon band will be slipped on her throat until she looks like a princess. Her feet are almost off the exquisite rug, jointly chosen from a lovely shop in the King's Road. A joint anniversary present, in fact. His right elbow swings up and back and he launches it at her left cheek. On impact, her head whips round and the right side of it bounces off the wall. It bounces back obediently and she is facing him again, waiting for her next instruction on how to live, who to be and whether she can exist at all. She awaits his command.

Her independent responses start her crying, and she sees both guilt and dismay in his eyes. This is the worst thing that can happen. Any sign that makes him consider that he could be a bully and a brute will make matters worse. He finds it easier not to have to consider the consequences of his behaviour. Tears make him realise he has upset her, why does she keep doing that? Playing the girl crying thing, confirming her weakness and his humanity.

He releases her and she wonders if her jaw has been dislocated, it feels as if it is clicking. He lies on the bed, aware that his friends are waiting for him. She is sitting on the carpet, collapsed on the spot he dropped her, trying to pretend she chose that random piece of floor of her own accord.

He tells her it will all be OK, not to cry. He appears to wonder why she is crying at all. She can hear soothing, warm words, that reassure her she is loved, it was all a big mistake, perhaps she deserved it. Maybe she imagined it.

He invites her to join him on the bed. She is wary, she

knows the fear is real, she feels frightened and is still crying. Her throat, neck, chin, cheek, jaw, head and legs hurt. Her stomach is knotted. He cajoles her like a hurt animal.

"It's OK, come on. I'm sorry. You know you shouldn't behave like that when my friends are here. You know I'm under stress. Why don't you just push me aside when I start to get a bit upset. You could stop it. It isn't anything really, not when you know how much I love you. Come on, let me give you a hug, let me comfort you. I can't bear to see you upset."

She slowly approaches the bed. She won't kill herself tonight, she won't go and join his friends, she won't go to family and friends who envy her idyllic life. She'll go to him. It'll be OK. Abuser becomes saviour. Role of victim not needed any more.

She sits on the bed, still wary. After all, she is an intelligent woman, with a heightened awareness of her own physical safety. She travels late on the Underground on her own. He coaxes, his voice is low and sensuous, the voice of her lover. She needs to be comforted, she has been through an ordeal. Slowly, slowly, she edges forward. With every inch she is rewarded with his soft kind voice, she longs to be comforted, who else to comfort her when no one else knows.

Their secret brings them closer. Two victims surviving together.

Closer still. Feeling better. It's over. Relief beats fear.

She is close enough to kiss him.

His hand snaps out like a flash. He has his hands round her throat. She hears threats.

She feels foolish. Should have known better.

He joins his friends.

She slowly slices at her arms, thighs and belly with the small fruit knife from the kitchen.

A female friend comes up the stairs. Someone who has never really liked her anyway but enjoys the role of being all-seeing, all-knowing. The friend tries to prise the duvet from over her head. She is stronger and has greater conviction. She is unsuccessful, but does glimpse a scrap of blood.

Self-inflicted.

It is up to her to make the abuse and physical pain a reality. She needs to see it, otherwise it doesn't really exist. He will say it didn't happen like that, what are you making a fuss for, always exaggerating.

The friend is whispering. She is saying that you all go through it. When she has confirmed it is natural to live this life, she leaves.

They all leave, and he wants to leave with them.

He comes upstairs and sees the most pitiful sight. She leans crouched against the radiator and begs him not to leave. She has hidden the keys to the car. He confirms how much he despises her, how every time she told him she didn't deserve happiness, she wasn't worthy, that this, in fact, was all true. Strangely enough he tells her every other partner he has had has also felt like this.

He leaves her and tells her he would do this again next time. If she attempts a serious suicide attempt, he will walk out and leave her like that. There is no other option.

It troubles him that she has this problem.

Tomorrow, she will return the Kitchen Devil to the cutlery drawer, wear a nice bracelet to cover her hacked-about arms and go about her responsible job, in which she is considered an exemplary employee, destined for great things.

MAYBE YOU DON'T believe this? Is he the type to be a violent bully who then looks for sympathy? Is she the type to self-harm and then protect him from others who might care?

You can't possibly know.
A night with friends in any flat with any couple in London.
Tomorrow we continue with our urban cool.

Nicola Barker

SALE

'BUT YOU'RE ALREADY *holding* a bag, Tony,' Lynsey patiently informs the immaculately attired Mr Anthony Banks-Wilder as he stands – chin aloft, shoulders back, eyes glinting – at the pharmacy counter.

Anthony Banks-Wilder (projecting absolute astonishment at this chit of a serving girl using his *Christian* name – worse still, in its abbreviated form) glances casually down at his emaciated hand which is firmly clutching (Ye *Gods!*) a small bag from Boots the Chemist (this compact Soho pharmacy's chief competitor).

He starts.

'Gracious me,' he exclaims.

Lynsey – with all the authority three GCSEs, a neat, white uniform and two years on the job can muster, and that's *plenty*, thank you very much – turns to try to serve another customer, a pasty-faced young girl with bad skin, a peach-coloured A-line skirt and an unassuming air.

'Can I help *you*, madam?' (note the emphasis – i.e. because I can't possibly help *him*).

The girl glances towards the old chap, deferentially. Her mouth opens. She gesticulates weakly. He's wearing *tweed*, after all (a wall of stinking, 80-degree city *heat* outside and he's dry as a nun's labia. Then there's the yellow waistcoat to contend with, the carnation button-hole, the colour-coordinated *cravat* . . .)

'But what business is it of *yours*,' ABW quickly butts in, lifting the bag haughtily, '*where* I've been shopping previously?'

'It's no business of ours,' the omnipresent pharmacist intones, in monochrome (a bored priest at the confessional), from behind his protective wall of pills and unguents.

'It's no business of ours,' Lynsey parrots obligingly.

'And anyway,' ABW continues smoothly, 'this is not *my* bag, it's my *neighbour's* bag. I'm simply looking after it for her.'

'Oh, really?'

Lynsey can't quite contain a tiny smirk.

'Yes,' ABW swipes the shuttle deftly back, 'really.'

Lynsey is unintimidated, 'Oh, *really*?' she reiterates (i.e. you bare-faced, duplicitous old *liar*).

ABW coolly maintains his poise *and* his serve, 'Yes' (but he flares his nostrils), '*really*.'

Impasse.

'Hmmn. Interesting. *Very* interesting . . .' Lynsey purses her lips and rubs her chin (a teenage Poirot with Ellesse trainers, lip gloss and a Krugerrand),'I wonder *which* of your neighbours that might be, exactly?'

'Which *neighbour*?'

ABW turns and gazes at the girl to his right – his lean but astonishingly tanned seventy-six-year-old face a picture of pained incredulity. 'Which *neighbour*?!'

'Lynsey . . .' the pharmacist intones warningly.

'Would that be Felicity *Burden* by any chance?' Lynsey persists (screw the pharmacist. He lives way out in leafy Surrey. What would he know?), 'or the messed-up black kid with the nappy hair and the Restraining Order?' (Lynsey is an all-seeing eye in this cosmopolitan enclave. The locals can't *fart* without her promptly investigating every how, why and wherefore.)

'*Eh?!*'

Nappy *what*?

ABW plays for time.

He double-blinks. He sniffs. He mugs. Lynsey doesn't move a muscle. She delivers him a straight stare.

ABW (on observing the exact nature of the stare – blunt and steadfast, with slight undertones of spleen and subtle notes of candour) hedges his bets and rapidly plumps for Mrs Burden.

'Felicity Burden,' he declares haughtily. '*Mrs* Burden to *you*, young lady.'

Lynsey's eyes tighten, infinitesimally.

'Could that possibly be,' she eventually hisses, leaning forward and resting her heavy forearms either side of the till, like a politician embracing the dispatch box (and sucking every inch of authority from its regal inanimateness), 'the *same* Mrs Burden who rushed in here late on Saturday to pick up a last-minute prescription for her two-week tour of Madagascar?'

Silence.

'*Madagascar?*' ABW finally gasps, as if place names possess tiny air-brakes and consequently take a little longer to reach him.

'Yup,' Lynsey intones smugly, 'Madagascar.'

'Mrs *Felicity* Burden?' ABW twitches (it's a big city out there, but in the cloistered hamlet of Soho even the damn *pigeons* are resolutely singular). Lynsey merely snorts. ABW twitches a second time, 'Well . . .' he jars, 'Well . . . then she can't possibly have *gone* yet, can she?'

They all know she's gone. The air conditioning, the strip lights, even the squeak in the newly polished floor tiles scream it: *Felicity Burden has gone to Madagascar. She went on bloody Sunday, you incorrigible bugger!*

'*Can* she, though?' ABW persists (cheerfully resolving to campaign against the evidence of all their senses).

Lynsey rolls her eyes.

Here we go.

'Because *if* she were in Madagascar,' ABW flutes (deciding to pepper his conversation with just a subtle *pinch* of poignant geriatric wobble for the benefit of the third unsuspecting customer who's just that second wandered in through the open door), '*how* could she have handed me this bag for safekeeping as we stood together – in front of the flower stall – not *five minutes* since?'

'Therein,' Lynsey opines sharply, 'lies the mystery.'

As luck would have it, however, ABW has cunningly chosen to address this perplexing philosophical query (on the fundamental nature of Mrs Felicity Burden's corporeal essence) *not* to Lynsey (screw Lynsey), but to the plain, young girl in the peach-coloured skirt. He tips his head (like some infernally scheming mynah bird), lifts a single, well-shaped brow, and politely awaits a response from her.

The girl smiles, apologetically. She isn't local. She isn't . . . 'I'm sorry, I'm not . . . I just work in a *bank*,' she explains plaintively.

Lynsey's eyes also flit over towards the peach-skirted girl. She isn't sure if she didn't go to school with her. In Epping. Lillian Walsh's kid sister. Three years younger.

'Can I help *you*, madam?' she asks breezily, for the second time.

'Uh . . .'

The girl takes a small step forward. Her name is Pauline

(she *did* go to school in Epping, as it so happens) and she is clutching some bubble bath, some toothpaste, some razor blades, some hair pins and an eye-liner.

'But you don't even *know* . . .' Anthony Banks-Wilder suddenly squawks, holding up the bag and shaking it defiantly, 'what I actually *have* in this bag. You can't possibly know. How *could* you?'

Lynsey doesn't bat an eyelid. 'Non-prescription painkillers,' she says, with absolute certainly.

'*Pardon?*'

ABW is – quite frankly – *astonished* by this guess.

'You heard me,' Lynsey mutters. The pharmacist coughs.

Pauline bites her lower lip and tentatively glances – through the veil of her lashes – towards the bag. It certainly *looks* (and sounds, from its distinctive rattle) like a packet of painkillers.

'But why on earth would I be buying painkillers?' ABW muses theatrically (to the empty dress circle), 'when I bought a packet in this very chemist only yesterday?'

'Why indeed?' Lynsey wonders (i.e. you pointless and disgusting, spaced-out old pill-popper).

'And anyway,' he continues (he's been called worse things in his time; *much* worse), 'I have *no idea* what this bag contains. This is Felicity's bag. My neighbour's bag. I wouldn't dream of looking inside my neighbour's bag. To do so would be a complete *breach* of the bond of confidence that she's placed in me.'

'Yeah,' Lynsey intones darkly, 'a bond so strong that it extends all the way over from the east coast of Africa.'

'I wouldn't *dream* of looking in the bag,' ABW reiterates, shaking the bag again, somewhat provocatively.

'OK . . . *OK*,' Lynsey rapidly resolves to call his bluff (this is a functioning *business*, after all, not some tragically under-resourced day care centre). 'So what do you actually intend on buying here today, Tony? A toothbrush? Some earbuds? A packet of *Lockets*, perhaps?'

She picks up a packet of Lockets and waggles it at him, invitingly.

ABW slowly lowers his Boots the Chemist bag and inclines his head, thoughtfully, 'Oh. *Uh*. Yes,' he ponders, 'Let's see . . .'

He scans the shelves awhile, nonchalantly, before his eye finally settles on the thing he most desires.

'A large box of Paracetamol, dearie,' he condescends, 'if you please.'

Lynsey stares at ABW, incredulously. ABW stares calmly back. The third person joins the queue and a fourth pops their head in through the door.

'*Disinfectant* . . .' she yells, 'D'you sell disinfectant?'

'For bodily application, yes,' the pharmacist pipes up, 'Top shelf. On your left.'

Ah.

'You know perfectly well, *Sir*,' Lynsey hisses, 'that we're only allowed to sell *one* packet of painkillers per customer per day. It's the law.'

'That's why I'm here,' ABW quavers, 'to get what's lawfully mine.'

'But you already *have* a packet, right there, in your hand. I can see the lettering on the box, quite clearly, through the plastic.'

'Vile lies,' ABW avers, 'and even if there *were* painkillers in this bag . . .' he waves the bag through the air again, 'and we have *no means* of knowing that for sure, then I certainly didn't buy them *here*.'

Now hang *on* there a second . . .

'But I thought *you* didn't buy them at all!' Lynsey trumps him.

Aw.

ABW is briefly trumped.

The third person in the queue (a man, in a rush, clutching a four-pack of tissues and apparently suffering from chronic hayfever) begins to grow impatient.

'Just give him the damn tablets, will you?' he sniffs, 'We're all in a hurry.'

'My sentiments entirely,' ABW echoes, with a smirk.

Lynsey gives the fourth man a stern look (filthy bastard. Runs the sex shop on Peter Street. Seems to be allergic to pretty much everything bar porn and sleaze and smut).

'You're right,' she concedes graciously, 'we're all in a hurry here. If Mr Banks-Wilder is so *determined* to overdose on non-prescription painkillers today, then why should *we* . . .' (she throws out her arms, inclusively), '. . . of all people, stand in his way?'

The pornographer grimaces.

'*Exactly,*' ABW concurs (somewhat counter-productively).

'Who needs stupid laws anyway?' Lynsey snorts.

The pharmacist – in the vain hope of defusing this situation – suddenly materialises at her side (perhaps a fraction grudgingly) to 'lend a hand'. He reaches out, matter-of-factly, to take Pauline's goods from her, and – as if liberated herself by his timely arrival – Lynsey reaches out, too, for the pornographer's tissues.

'One pound twenty-five, please,' she says, and pops them into a bag. The pornographer passes her one pound thirty. She hands him his purchase and then awaits her turn on the till.

ABW (abandoned, shunted, *rail*roaded) is not happy. He is *un*happy. He draws a sharp breath. He slits his eyes, and then, '*Excuse* me, my dear,' he says, reaching over – with two raptorial digits – and pinching at the unsuspecting Pauline's sleeve.

Ouch!

She glances up, with a jump, from her bag (where she's currently rummaging, searching for her purse).

'Sorry?'

'How *old* are you, my darling?' ABW purrs.

She blinks.

The pharmacist, meantime, is already ringing through the bubble bath (Radox, herbal), the hair pins and the kohl. He's grappling with the toothpaste . . .

'How old?' ABW persists. 'Your *age*, my love.'

Pauline frowns. 'Uh . . . Seven . . . seventeen,' she stutters, 'I'm seventeen.'

'*STOP!*' Anthony Banks-Wilder bellows.

Everybody stops (even the people who aren't actually doing anything).

'Razors,' ABW points at the offending objects (a handy pack of six, cut-throat, currently clutched between the pharmacist's fingers), 'cannot be purchased by anyone under eighteen years of age.'

Pauline looks alarmed, then shocked, then embarrassed, 'But I'll be . . . I'll be eighteen in a week,' she gabbles, 'Well,' she pauses, frantically calculating, 'a week and three days . . .'

ABW shrugs, 'The law is the law is the law,' he sighs.

The transaction is duly halted.

'*Bollocks*,' the pornographer curses, turning and heading for the door, abandoning his change.

Lynsey's jaw stiffens. She mashes her lips together. She tightens her fist (his money still in her hand). The pharmacist continues hesitating.

'I'd *hate* to be the cause of any bother . . .' Pauline murmurs, both cheeks flushing deeply.

'Don't be silly,' Lynsey interrupts her, 'it's nothing. It's *fine*. It's simply a matter of . . . of professional *discretion* . . .'

'Ah,' ABW mutters poignantly, nodding his head towards the fourth customer (who's just that second joined them), 'One law for the *young*, eh?'

He hangs his old head down, apparently broken.

The fourth customer (a brash but kind-hearted lady fish-monger) immediately grows indignant on his behalf.

'That does seem a little tough,' she interjects, glaring at the pharmacist.

ABW merely shrugs, 'Where's the point in fighting it?' he hoarsely ponders, then winces, putting out a frail and shaking hand to support his lower spine.

'*Sciatica* . . .' he silently mouths.

Lynsey gasps.

The pharmacist is still holding the razors aloft, almost in horror, like they're a small, live mouse, suspended by its tail.

'It'd be wrong,' he tells Lynsey, 'purely as a matter of *business*, to be seen to be employing double standards . . .'

'It's absolutely OK, *really* . . .' Pauline quickly interrupts, 'I don't need them. I'll leave them. I'll just . . . I'll just *pay* . . .' She finds her purse and opens it. She takes out a handful of money.

'I'll tell you what,' the fishmonger suddenly weighs in (she's in retail herself, she *understands* the pressures). 'How about if *I* buy the painkillers and then . . .'

'Absolutely *not*.'

Lynsey and the pharmacist speak with one voice.

ABW's ears prick up. His eyes glimmer. He senses an opportunity.

'But what if she was intending to buy some anyway?' he asks innocently, 'for *herself*?'

'She wasn't,' Lynsey snaps, 'she isn't. She came in for disin-fectant.'

'*Did* I?' The fishmonger (not appreciating Lynsey's tone) immediately jerks her chin up.

'I'll just . . .' Pauline is blindly piling money on to the counter, 'just *pay* . . .'

'One packet of painkillers, please!' The fishmonger's voice rings out, defiantly.

'. . . and then . . . then *go*.'

As Pauline places the final coin on to the countertop, the cuff of her linen shirt slips down, revealing three thick, white slashes – smooth tracks of shiny sugar icing – across her wrist.

ABW's eyes widen. The pharmacist blanches. Lynsey falters.

Pauline rapidly yanks the cuff back into place.

'Did you *hear* me?' the fishmonger asks.

'Yes. *Yes*,' Pauline whispers, almost flinching, 'We all heard.'

The pharmacist totals up the till, piles Pauline's other items into a bag, and places the razors (very gently but firmly) to one side. He passes the bag over. She snatches it and holds it to her chest, breathing deeply, as he sorts out her money. He takes what he needs and leaves the rest.

Lynsey, meanwhile, has turned and grabbed a small packet of Anadin from the shelf behind her.

'Allergic!' ABW pipes up.

'Not those!' the fishmonger barks.

She sullenly places them back.

The pharmacist gives Pauline her receipt. Pauline shoves it into her purse, murmurs a muted thank you, then heads for the door.

She's left her change.

'She's left her change,' the pharmacist mutters.

'Here . . .' Lynsey shoves the pack of Paracetamol over the counter at ABW. 'You win. Well *done*. Five other big chemists in the immediate area . . .,' she grabs Pauline's change, 'but for some strange reason you always come back to *us* . . .'

She ducks under the counter, 'I mean, anyone might start to think . . .,' she mutters softly, cruelly, as she emerges on the other side and brushes by him, 'that you were simply addicted to the *fuss*.'

LYNSEY CATCHES UP with Pauline in the street, just adjacent to the chip shop.

'Forgot your change,' she pants, touching her shoulder.

Pauline spins around. She seems disorientated.

'Oh God,' she says, remembering, 'My *change*. Thank you. Sorry.'

She takes the change.

'Here . . .' Lynsey offers her something else.

Pauline blinks.

'Take them,' Lynsey says, 'On me.' She grins, 'It's all a matter of *discretion*, see?'

Then she nods at the boy on the fruit stall, winks at Pauline, and heads back off.

Pauline gazes down at the razors, blankly, her mind running and re-running – like a malfunctioning computer – through all the meticulous details of the evening she'd planned. Then she throws the rest of her shopping into a nearby waste bin, pauses for a second, shuts her eyes, inhales, and slowly – *slowly* – shakes her young, dull head, holding those six sharp blades, very tightly, in her hand.

Fran Hill

BEING 'MISS'

TWO DAYS BEFORE the US and Britain start trying to bomb Saddam Hussein out of existence, a boy in my Year 8 class at the Wimbledon school where I'm doing my teaching practice glances at his watch and asks me, quite casually, 'Miss, what time is the war starting?'

In the split-second before I realise what he's referring to, I wonder how he found out that I've got that bottom set I'm terrified of in Period 3 and I nearly reply, 'Just after break, Justin. Pray for me.' But then I catch on. He's talking about Iraq, and he's still looking up at me, trusting that I will know the answer.

'I don't think anyone knows what time it will start, Justin. In fact, it's probably not even going to be today.'

This seems to satisfy him. He pulls his sleeve back down over his watch and walks into class. If I'd said '10.36 our time' I have a feeling he was going to set his alarm to go off in the middle of Geography, so it's just as well I didn't know.

Following him and twenty-nine others into the room, I wonder for the thousandth time whether I can cope with this teaching lark. It's too much of a burden, being expected to *know* things. No one else among my family and friends would ever come with a question about current affairs and expect me to give the answer. The sense of responsibility that comes with being 'Miss' is almost too much to bear. It occurs to me that Justin, a small boy with round spectacles and a few intelligent freckles on the bridge of his nose, probably knows a damn sight more about the war than I do. I make a mental note to keep out of his way unless it's a question about apostrophes. I'm good on apostrophes. I can even write about the war using the correct apostrophes. Look. *The Americans have bombs. They are the Americans' bombs.* See. Justin may have his head stuffed with current affairs but I bet he'd have put that apostrophe before the 's', if he'd used one at all.

As I give out the exercise books, I suppress a sneaking feeling that knowing where to put an apostrophe isn't one of life's priorities when there's a war on, but somehow this morning it helps. Heaven knows, I need all the help I can get.

KNOWING ABOUT APOSTROPHES isn't all good. Sometimes, when I'm wandering around the city, the high street or the park, jabbing my finger impatiently at all the misplaced or missing apostrophes in posters and signs and local byelaws, I wonder why I have been given this particular talent. For a start, it isolates one at parties. Mention a passion for the correctly sited apostrophe at a party and you might as well have asked: 'Anyone else having problems with excess wind?' You are a social pariah, a person whom people steer clear of, whom no one will ever write to again for fear that you keep a spreadsheet on your friends' apostrophe errors and update it nightly before you go to bed.

Chance would be a fine thing. Since starting my teacher training I wouldn't have had time to keep an apostrophe spreadsheet if I'd wanted to (and I don't want to – I think). It might have been an interesting exercise to do while practising for my compulsory Government Key Skills ICT test, and some of the material on that is nearly as exciting as apostrophes, but I wouldn't have had time. Evenings are spent doing lesson plans, evaluating lessons, writing up observations of lessons, crossing out things I've written about other teachers that they might get to see, writing lists of things to do although I know I've done this already somewhere but I can't remember where, and filling in forms that ask me to find out school policy on numeracy, SEN policy, health and safety and the name of the head's secretary's aunt's cousin's granny. Now there's a run of apostrophes to be proud of.

AT THE BUS STOP on the way home that afternoon, I feel a bit panicky. Waiting for the same bus, what seems like a hundred shuffling, kicking and swearing boys push and shove, not maliciously, but just in an end-of-school-day-and-aren't-we-grateful kind of way. Their school uniforms fall into disarray before my very eyes, crisps and chewing gum appear from every pocket and all the Walkmans and mobiles they are not even supposed to bring to school are hissing and beeping. Every now and again, a boy falls into the busy road, sometimes voluntarily, sometimes pushed, and a car has to brake.

At that moment, I wish I wasn't a teacher at their school, albeit only a student one. I wish I didn't recognise some of them. I wish, I really wish, I didn't know that they were breaking every rule in the Code of Behaviour Outside School section of their school planner, including the one about eating on the way to and from school.

Just as I am thinking this, one of my Year 8s nudges another whom I don't teach and says in a stage whisper that would have reached to the back of the upper circle, 'Sssh. That's Mrs Hill, one of the teachers.' They both giggle and the other boy looks up at me. He's seen me at this bus stop several times. 'Sorry, Miss,' he says. 'I never knew you was a teacher. I thought you was a normal person.' I raise my eyebrows. 'No, Miss. I didn't mean it to be rude. I mean, I thought you was just a public.'

I smile benevolently. 'I'm a teacher and a public,' I tell him.

I hope any parents reading this will be relieved to know that when students make mistakes in their grammar and vocabulary, they are quickly and efficiently corrected by committed teachers anxious to make sure that they grow up being able to talk proper.

The bus hasn't arrived yet and now some of the boys are running a spitting competition to see who can gob as far as the white lines in the middle of the road. Suddenly a male teacher appears from nowhere to check behaviour at the bus stop. I didn't notice him coming and certainly the boys didn't. While he deals with the boys, brisk and confident like the real teacher I know I'm not yet, I shuffle to the back of the long queue, turn my back and hope he doesn't recognise me. Turned the wrong way like that, there's a danger I'm not going to see the bus coming and it will go without me, but it's a price worth paying. It also means they can all get their crisps and mobiles out again once they're on the bus and chomp and beep in peace without me there to feel guilty about watching them do it.

This just shows that I don't yet have the mean streak I know I will have to develop if I'm going to get anywhere in this job. It's all very well reading Bill-Rogers-the-discipline-guru on a Friday evening and vowing never to let Bobby get away with flicking spit-laden pellets at Richie again. Come Monday morning, I tend to agree with Bobby that Richie is a pain in the bum and that, although flicking spit-laden pellets isn't the method I would choose, he deserves something horrible to happen to him. It's all very well me committing the chapter on Establishing Rules to memory; it's another thing having the courage to eyeball someone who's 6 foot 3 and the captain of the rugby team and tell them they've got yet another detention for not doing homework. Eyeballing them in the first place is difficult when you're only 5 foot 2 yourself. He could, I suppose, always claim that I only gave his navel a detention and as it was difficult to send just the navel along on its own to write 'I will always do my homework' a hundred times, he decided not to bother.

BEING SHORT is almost as much of a handicap in teaching as not knowing much about current affairs. It's just as well I don't know loads about current affairs, seeing as I can only utilise a third of the whiteboard to write stuff up there anyway. I mean, I can't even reach to change the date most days – and that's about as current as things get – unless I stand on a chair. I'm the only student teacher in London who has to lash the board rubber on to the end of the window-pole with a rubber band and it's not funny. For a start, I have to borrow a rubber band from a child because I never remember my own, and as they're not supposed to have these on them, this rather undermines the school rules. Secondly, it takes five minutes of the lesson to get the board rubber/window-pole organised, so I feel I ought to include it in my lesson plan, but can I find a National Curriculum objective *anywhere* to write against this activity? Can I heck. It isn't mentioned anywhere. It just goes to show that the Government knows *nothing* about what happens in classrooms these days and when my tutor points out the omission in my file, the Education Secretary can take all the blame.

I HOP OFF THAT BUS and hurry to my next bus stop, hoping I see no more students. No such luck. There, waiting for the same bus as me, are three lads I teach, all clutching paper cones overflowing with chips. This is as blatant a breach of school rules as one can get and somehow the crime of stuffing hot steaming chips seems a lot worse than chewing a few sweets or a lolly. And anyway, I'm bloody starving and beginning to salivate.

'What do you think you're doing?' I glare at them, hoping that I look scary. 'You know it's strictly forbidden to be seen eating while you're in uniform. This is a serious offence.'

They look repentant, but only just. And I can't think what to do about it anyway. As much as I'd love to, I can't confiscate three bags of chips, can I? Not without providing free entertainment to the increasingly interested queue of passengers. I could make them throw them away, but I have a feeling I might end up in court. Parents aren't what they used to be.

'I'll be reporting this to your Head of Year,' I tell them, making a mental note to find out who it is. 'You'd better not do it again.'

'No, Miss,' they chorus, and stand looking at me, wondering what I'm going to do next. Then one cheeky sod holds out his chips. These kids are brighter than they look. 'D'you want one, Miss? They're lovely and hot.'

'No, I do *not* want one. Now go and stand over there, away from people waiting. Not everyone wants your smelly chips around them.'

If only this were true. I not only want to smell them, I want to rush into the fried chicken shop where they bought theirs and buy a giant cone for myself, salted and vinegared and the best taste in the world when you haven't eaten since breaktime. But how can I?

This is teaching for you, Mrs Hill, I tell myself, and it serves you right for being so arrogant about your apostrophes. Never again will you be able to lean against a bus stop in daylight hours, cramming chips into your mouth, or Mars bars, or your favourite pink candy shrimps, or anything more incriminating than a Tic-Tac. Not only that, but you can never pick your nose in the car within forty miles of where you're working, or slob around town in baggy jeans and the jumper you slept in.

At this moment, with the aroma of chip still wafting cruelly in front of my nostrils, I feel like trading in a whole teaching career, apostrophe talent notwithstanding, for a bag of greasy potatoes. But what stops me throwing caution to the winds is thinking back to what a small boy said half an hour ago. Would I really want to give up this roller-coaster, nausea-inducing, stomach-churning ride they call teacher training to return to those uneventful days of being 'just a public'?

The bus arrives. The three chip-eaters have discarded their rubbish, in the bin thankfully, otherwise I'd have had something else to deal with, and stand back respectfully to let me on first. Before I can stop myself, I'm smiling at them and raising my eyebrows conspiratorially. They grin. They know as well as I do that the news of their crime is never going to reach the Head of Year, and it probably also guarantees that they'll play up in their next lesson with me. I shake my head at them to show my deep disappointment in their behaviour, but the battle is lost.

The mean streak, it is clear, is taking a while to develop.

Diran Adebayo

P IS FOR POST-BLACK

HE'S IN A RUSH. And a mood. Annoyed with himself, and with all these people clogging up the escalators at Leicester Square. You know, the idiots and the tourists standing on the wrong side, just all the people. And thinking, 'I can't believe this. First date, and I'm late.'

Out in the evening air, and only his agitation prevents a full-on attack of the grumps. There's the usual confusion about which way to head because both sides of the Charing Cross Road look the same to him. Always have. A late-twenties Londoner and he's still not got to grips with this West End thing.

Everything just blends: a blending heave of side streets and shoppers and euros and Americans and lagered provincials down for their capital city crack; leisurely hordes, almost all non-Londoners, all impeding his way. He looks both ways, then remembers that the side with the downward slope takes you to Trafalgar. He turns and, grumpier still, starts uphill.

Force-marching a foot or so in the road, the better to avoid human traffic, he's greeted by some new sights among the old. First, a black guy, seriously the worse for wear, who reels into him off the kerb. 'Sorry, mate!' says the brother, before stumbling back to his white boys, and he's surprised to hear a London accent rather than country tones. Surprised too by the apology, which found him with a scowl in place.

Wow! he smiles to himself. That's the first time, maybe in his life, he's seen one of his kind properly pissed in public. Not holding it down. For shame! And Londoner too. He'll know the blacks to know better. No excuses.

Further on, and there are more instances of unorthodox black behaviour: a black-and-white couple, the black lady's arm elegantly, continentally, linked around his, on a stroll, stopping by the odd venue or store window, promenading. A pack of young women on a night out, a mixed bunch, all grouped around a bar table, a few clothes bags at their side. Happy with themselves; glugging Bacardi breezers and enjoying the booming economy. Not posh-black or those slightly freaky Soho types, just regular, neighbourhood-looking girls, being mainstream. Sort of . . . post-black.

He wonders why he's not so happy for them; not smiling encouragingly at these post-blacks. He wanted that too, he couldn't deny . . . To . . . to break free from the restrictive codes of black-britdom. Hunh. Wasn't that what he'd been doing, student bar-crawling in the first place? Trying to find a black girl at a good, old university: some quality, new-breed black girl who was spending her socially formative years in the company of natives and might therefore have a looser, 'whiter', vibe . . . What had brought him here, on a Saturday, to Leicester Square?

A writer by profession and bohemian by heart, he'd been finding the black circles he mixed in more and more stifling, Like this house party the other day. There were various guys there he knew from various other dos and, as usual, they nodded to each other and said, 'All right. How's it going?' then nodded once more then stood by one another a little while, each with a bottle of Becks, and that was pretty much it. Everyone stands and looks quite good, and holds it down and

sways coolly to the odd tune, but no one actually talks. No
incidents, no deep chats, no real flirting; no one gets embar-
rassingly happy, gets anything big or different out of it. No . .
. secrets to be found there. True, he didn't want people banging
into him, and vomiting by his feet or something, as happened
at many white dos, but he could do with a little more loose-
ness. Huh. The big lie about us, he thinks, is that we're wild.

*At SOAS bar I met him. My college is Birkbeck, down the
road, but I used to go to the SOAS one 'cos they've got a pool
table and he saw me playing pool, beating these guys. I think
he liked that! Anyway, after, I was sat down, headphones on –
I didn't hang out with the pool posse or anything, just played
– and I was reading when this guy wanders over and stops by
me. I didn't take him in too closely. He looked a bit trendy –
you know, zip-up top, one of those beanie hats – and trendies
don't normally do me. I'm just a maths chick from the country.*

*He all but snatches this book from me, and starts flipping
through it, firing me these questions: simultaneous, quadratic
equations, 'What are they for?' It was nice, you know, his little
science queries. Most arty types think they're so superior, that
their stuff is so much more interesting, it gets on my tits.*

*He mentioned quite a bit of black stuff as well. It didn't
surprise me – up here, I'd noticed, blacks talk about black stuff
a lot. Normally . . . well, normally, it's dreary but he was quite
funny with it. Like this rant about how most black students
weren't studying anything serious. If anything it was all these
mickey-mouse mixy-mixy modular courses: 'media an' this',
and 'crap an' communication studies', and everyone wanted to
be some silly TV presenter and it was so nice to meet someone
doing a proper subject.*

And I remember priming myself then not to say 'half-caste'

or 'coloured', words that have got me into moments up here.
So I must have quite liked him already.

I gave him my number. I didn't think he'd call.

SOMETHING . . . spirited and particular about her. Walkman on in a bar! Maths and classical music. Indifferent, too. The way she was beating those stoners at pool. They were nattering, trying to banter, and she was acknowledging just enough, unconcealed unconcern on her face, the same wider unconcern that she carried with her in her busy movements around the table, a similar indifference in the eyes that looked through the boy who was looking at her.

He had been beguiled by this indifference. He had seen Africa, the Africa of his family, and his yearnings, in the style of this light-skinned, evidently yellow girl: like the plainly dressed waitresses at Mama Calabar's in Hendon as they stood by the tables; or the looks on young women in London or Lagos sashaying down the street with a languid, stately, posterior-pouting sway of the hips, knowing, seeing but not seeing you.

You weren't sure she liked you. He liked that. Didn't say much, after he'd approached. Just stared most of the time, then burst in with something odd.

Her look too. An unstyled wildness to the hair, big Ibo cheeks, hint of chinie about the eyes. 'Where are you from?' he'd asked her. 'It's a long story,' she'd replied. 'Another time.' And when he'd pressed, she'd smiled shyly and laughed, 'The future.'

The future!

He sees the little left he is looking for, Hunt Court, and turns into it, passing another mixed couple. The black girl gives him the merest glance; unimpressed, indifferent. He knows that look – you got it often from blackheads in groups or couples like that in arty Shoreditch, his sometime stomping ground. The look said that they did not associate, could not imagine having such a modern, free time with people like you. Maybe that's the problem, he decides, as he runs the last few yards: sometimes, it seems, he fears, that in this post-black future, black on black won't be happening.

He'd said to meet in the World Music section in Virgin Records near Leicester Square, which was nice and quiet, but by the time he came, twenty minutes late, I'd wandered up to the Classical floor, so it was a little smart of him to find me.

He was more elegantly dressed this time – pleated black trousers, suede green jacket, only he looked as if he'd looked better a bit before. His forehead was beading with sweat. From running, I imagined. He kept on dabbing it with this manky tissue, leaving little white flecks behind. Maybe if I'd looked away he would have done it properly.

It was rush-rush to Rupert Street round the corner for the cinema. The film – that was mad! Spanking the Monkey, *this offbeat, non-Hollywood production. Canadian, I think. It was about this teenage guy with issues who spent most of his time either wanking or having sex with his Mum, maybe it was his stepmother. He glanced round the odd time to ask if it was all right, if I was enjoying it. I nodded.*

He seemed quite embarrassed after: 'Ah, Lordy! They said in the paper it was a – not a "black comedy", I know what that means – but, you know, a black indie drama or something. I thought it was gonna have Afros!'

He wanted to take me next to this bar he was a member of on Charing Cross Road. The bar had a late licence which was why he was a member. It was nothing much, he said, just a pub really, but the vibe was nice; actors an' comedians an' such frequented it.

Only we, he, couldn't find it. Rupert Street to Charing Cross Road is about six hundred yards if you do it right. Do it wrong, and fifteen minutes are gone and you're still walking. I did make a suggestion at one point but he didn't take it. He kept apologising, saying we'd be there in a minute. He was sweating again.

I was fine. I thought it quite funny, him being a Londoner.

I think it was then I first thought, tissue flecks back on his forehead, eyes screwing at street signs, 'You're quite dizzy, aren't you?' Maybe not those words exactly, but that was my thought.

We ended up somehow on Maiden Lane by Covent Garden. He stood strong again. He knew this top bar here, The Spot; said we should try that instead.

It had this big glass frontage, and this black bouncer, then another one we passed to reach a second bar inside. I was happy there from the off, not for the stylish decor or stylish people, but for the cocktails they were drinking. I'm a cocktail fiend, only you don't get much chance to indulge on a student's debts and I knew he would ask and get me one – I hadn't dipped in my pocket since we'd met.

He was reaching down to his when the barman set down our chemical colours, turned and walked away. A puzzled brow at me, then at the crowd thickening around us, then a beam:

'It's a do! Some celebo do! You know who that is?'

He looked a teeny bit familiar: a boxer or footballer. But the main guy, whose do it was, I definitely recognised. He was upstairs, in the dancing room we drifted up to. He played for Arsenal or Man United, one of those. Scored their goals. He had a smoking jacket on, his hair in cornrows, and a busty blondie beside him. There were a lot of blondes, a lot of light-skinned girls. In thigh-split dresses and clingy things and glossy hair – it was serious high-maintenance in there. But most of them didn't properly look classy. They looked a bit like the girls you could see back home when they put their Friday night faces on. So even though it was this upscale place, and this famous guy's birthday party, I didn't feel intimidated.

We clinked glasses and I felt clever and naughty, part of a little Zombie conspiracy. Zombies – rum and liqueurs, that's my favourite. He tried one too, one among all these other glasses on the go. Mad! He had, like, three or four at any one time – a Zombie, a brandy, a Baileys and some tea, and he'd go from one to the other, cold then hot then cold again, sip, slurp. And none of them ever finished.

I was glad for these little things, the drinks and the dizzy things. I think otherwise he might have been too . . . you know, trendy for me. But these made him better, softer. Soft-toned, baby's dimples. Soft, I was thinking. Quite a sweetboy.

A GUEST walks past them who looks like Denzel Washington. He asks her if she thinks Denzel Washington is sexy. 'No,' she shakes her head. 'He's like a stone.' 'A stone!' 'Yeah. Not . . . alive to me. Like a nice picture. A stone.'

He smiles quizzically at her: this . . . funny girl who's brought him luck tonight; who was cool as he faffed about on the street before. Who says things like Denzel Washington is a stone.

We made most of our important discoveries that night; how I was adopted; how we both liked chess. Oh, he told me why he'd laughed when I'd said we could meet Saturday. He said he couldn't believe I'd allowed Saturday, that he hadn't been given a first date Saturday since his Stone Age. Most of the girls he knew, even if they checked for you, they'd allow a first date midweek lunch, or else a drink after work. Maybe third or fourth you'd get a weekend rendezvous.

'You don't play games. It's good,' he grinned.

And other stuff, for sure, but I don't recall so much of it 'cos I was pretty giddy by the time we left, with the drink and the hormones of it all. I felt fine when we were sat inside but then outside – whoosh! Little Miss Mashed, that was me.

We nearly got a cab back – there were those illegal ones outside. But I feared another change in atmosphere – the staleness and motion of a car, and it might be all off. So we walked. It wasn't so far, and I'm pretty brisk, even at the pissed of times.

He says he asked, 'So what kind of guys d'you like?' and I exclaimed, 'Headfucks!' or 'Guys who can headfuck. Like chess, like maths is a headfuck!' And he started something concerned about how it must have been tough, growing up mixed in the sticks, till I burst in, 'I like "coloured". Why not "coloured"? Like a palette. We're the colours, they're not!'

And I threw my arms, he said, at the lights from a store window. I probably had the cocktails in mind too. I don't recall, only the sight of him, stopped, some paces behind, by a shop, looking at me this way he does when he exclaims my name sometimes, this intrigued, indulgent look, and me, peacefully tingly, deep feeling he doesn't mind how I'm different.

FOR ONE MOMENT, as she bounds in front of him, he has an echo of the drunkard before, but this time he doesn't mind. Her boyish, busy walk reminds him of someone from *Buffy*, one of those kick-ass slayers, and he christens her Miss P: Miss

P for pool and her kind of punky, undomesticated vibe. A bit backward, bit rustic maybe, on certain issues, but that would be sorted down the line.

It feels right that they dated first in Leicester Square, in this in-between land that neither of them owned, this anything-goes square mile that was neither country nor neighbourhood, this irritating turf that has finally come through for him . . . Oh Miss P, Miss P, he beams at her, I'm gonna have a sweet post-black time with you.

ABOUT THE AUTHORS

Diran Adebayo's first novel, *Some Kind of Black* (1996), was longlisted for the Booker Prize and won the Saga Prize, a Betty Trask award, the Authors' Club's Best First Novel Award and the Writers' Guild's New Writer of the Year Award. He is currently working on his third novel, *Dizzy and Miss P*.

Nicola Barker won the 1993 David Higham Award for Fiction, and was the joint winner of the Macmillan Silver Pen Award for Fiction with *Love your Enemies*. Her novel *Wide Open* (1998) won the Dublin IMPAC Award; *Clear* was longlisted for the 2004 Man Booker Prize.

Saeed Taji Farouky, born in Epsom of Egyptian/Palestinian background, is a journalist and documentary film-maker who lived in the Middle East before settling in London fifteen years ago. He is a regular contributor to *Sharq*, the UK's bestselling arts and culture magazine for British Arabs.

Romesh Gunesekera was born in Sri Lanka and has lived in London for many years. His first novel *Reef* was shortlisted for the 1994 Booker Prize; *Heaven's Edge* was listed as a 2003 New York Times Notable Book. His other books are *The Sandglass* and *Monkfish Moon*.

Sarah Hall was born in Cumbria in 1974. Her novel *Haweswater* (2002) won the Commonwealth Best First Novel Prize and a Betty Trask award; *The Electric Michangelo* was shortlisted for the Man Booker Prize and longlisted for the Orange Prize in 2004.

Fran Hill trained to teach English after years of working in the NHS. She now teaches full-time in Richmond-upon-Thames. She writes, reads, visits the theatre and cinema – and plays the guitar until her children beg her to stop.

Louise Hocking was born in 1963 in London. She currently lives in West London and is studying at the Chelsea College of Art and Design.

Hanif Kureishi received an Oscar nomination for his first screenplay, *My Beautiful Laundrette* (1984). *The Buddha of Suburbia* (1990) won the Whitbread First Novel Award; his first short story collection, *Love in a Blue Time*, was published in 1997.

Andrea Levy was born in London to Jamaican parents. She is the author of four novels: *Every Light in the House Burnin'* (1994), *Never Far from Nowhere* (1996), *Fruit of the Lemon* (1999) and *Small Island*, which won both the Orange Prize for Fiction and Whitbread Book of the Year in 2004, and the 2005 Commonwealth Writers' Prize.

Max Mueller, trained as a toolmaker, left his native Germany in 1990 after refusing military service, and now lives in London. His previous writing includes *Mars Flight* (2004), with Alasdair Mangham, for BBC Radio 4.

Patrick Neate is the author of *Musungu Jim*, which won a Betty Trask award, and *Twelve Bar Blues*, which won the National Book Critics' Circle of America Prize for criticism. His latest novel is *City of Tiny Lights* (due June 2005).

Paul T. Owen was born in Manchester in 1978. He studied at Sheffield, Pittsburgh and the London School of Economics, and lives in London where he works as a journalist. He is working on his first novel.

Shereen Pandit was a lawyer and law lecturer, trade unionist and political activist in South Africa and the UK before she turned to writing in 1996. Her short stories have won several competitions.

Alex Wheatle, born in South London of Jamaican parents, made a name for himself as 'the Brixton Bard'. His novels *Brixton Rocks*, *East of Acre Lane* and *Seven Sisters* were received with great acclaim. His latest novel is *Island Songs* (due July 2005).

THE GLORIOUS FLIGHT OF PERDITA TREE

Also available from
THE MAIA PRESS

UNITY
Michael Arditti

Michael Arditti's fourth novel examines the personalities and politics involved in the making of a film about the relationship between Unity Mitford and Hitler, set against the background of the Red Army Faction terror campaign in 1970s Germany. Almost thirty years after the film had to be abandoned following its leading actress's participation in a terrorist attack, the narrator sets out to uncover her true motives – by exploring her relationships with her aristocratic English family, the German *wunderkind* director, a charismatic Palestinian activist, her university boyfriend, a former Hollywood child star and an Auschwitz survivor turned high-powered pornographer.

Unity paints a deeply disturbing picture of corruption and fanaticism in both Britain and Germany from the 1930s to the present day. Startlingly original, this remarkable novel is a profound exploration of the nature of evil.
'A wonderful novel, written with exceptional knowledge and understanding of past and present Germany'—Gitta Sereny

£8.99 ISBN 1 904559 12 3

THE GLORIOUS FLIGHT OF PERDITA TREE
Olivia Fane

Perdita Tree, the bored and beautiful wife of Tory MP Nicholas Hodgekin, believes that all married women, and perhaps all women everywhere, should have a magic door through which they can walk into a different life – 'utterly, utterly different, not necessarily better, just something other'. So when she is kidnapped in Albania, she takes it in the spirit of one huge adventure. Adored by her kidnapper, who believes all things English are perfect, she is persuaded to rescue the Albanians from their dire history, and is vain enough to imagine that she can. Together they ride across the country on horseback, singing Beatles songs and preaching freedom. The year is 1991, democracy is coming, but are the Albanians ready for it? And are they ready for Perdita?

With this beguiling novel, Olivia Fane considers the nature of love, longing and betrayal and, above all, the art of being free.
'This book is a delight ... I loved it. .... It races along at a rate of knots, leaving the reader smiling, satisfied and impressed'—Fay Weldon

£8.99 ISBN 1 904559 13 1

OCEANS OF TIME Merete Morken Andersen

'Artistry and
intensity of vision'—
Guardian
'An intensely moving
novel'—
Independent
£8.99
ISBN 1 904559 11 5

A long-divorced couple face a family tragedy in
the white night of a Norwegian summer. Forced
to confront what went wrong in their relationship,
they plumb the depths of sorrow and despair before
emerging with a new understanding. This profound
novel deals with loss and grief, but also,
transformingly, with hope, recovery and love.
Translated from Norwegian by Barbara J. Haveland
LONGLISTED FOR INDEPENDENT FOREIGN FICTION PRIZE 2005
WINNER OF THE NORWEGIAN CRITICS' AWARD 2003

ESSENTIAL KIT Linda Leatherbarrow

'Full of acute
observation,
surprising imagery
and even shocks ...
joyously surreal ...
gnomically funny,
and touching'—
Shena Mackay
£8.99
ISBN 1 904559 10 7

In these varied and exquisite short stories, Linda
Leatherbarrow brings together for the first time her
prize-winning short prose with new and previously
unpublished work. A wide-ranging, rich and surprising
gallery of characters includes a nineteen-year-old girl
leaving home, a talking gorilla in the swinging sixties,
a shoe fetishist and a long-distance walker. The prose
is lyrical, witty and uplifting, funny and moving,
always pertinent – proving that the short story is the
perfect literary form for contemporary urban life.

RUNNING HOT Dreda Say Mitchell

'An exciting new
voice in urban
fiction'—*Guardian*
'Swaggeringly cool
and incredibly funny
... maintains a
cracking pace' —
Stirling Observer
£8.99
ISBN 1 90455909 3

Elijah 'Schoolboy' Campbell is heading out of
London's underworld, a world where bling, ringtones
and petty deaths are accessories of life. He's taking a
great offer to leave it all behind and start a new life,
but the problem is he's got no spare cash. He stumbles
across a mobile phone, but it is marked property, and
the Street won't care that he found it by accident.
And the door to redemption is only open for seven
days ... Schoolboy knows that when you're running
hot, all it takes is one phone call or one text message
to disconnect you from this life – permanently. Dreda
Say Mitchell was born into London's Grenadian
community. This is her first novel.

GOOD CLEAN FUN Michael Arditti

'Witheringly funny,
painfully acute'—
Literary Review
'A simply
outstanding
collection'—
City Life, Manchester
£8.99
ISBN 1 904559 08 5

This dazzling first collection of short stories from an award-winning author employs a host of remarkable characters and a range of original voices to take an uncompromising look at love and loss in the twenty-first century. These twelve stories of contentment and confusion, defiance and desire, are marked by wit, compassion and insight. Michael Arditti was born in Cheshire and lives in London. He is the author of three highly acclaimed novels, *The Celibate*, *Pagan and her Parents* and *Easter*.

A BLADE OF GRASS Lewis DeSoto

'A plangent debut
... an extremely
persuasive bit of
storytelling'
—*Daily Mail*
'Outstanding debut
novel' —*The Times*
£8.99
ISBN 1 904559 07 7

Märit Laurens farms with her husband near the border of South Africa. When guerrilla violence and tragedy visit their lives, Märit finds herself in a tug of war between the local Afrikaaners and the black farmworkers. Lyrical and profound, this exciting novel offers a unique perspective on what it means to be black and white in a country where both live and feel entitlement. DeSoto, born in South Africa, emigrated to Canada in the 1960s. This is his first novel.
LONGLISTED FOR THE MAN BOOKER PRIZE 2004
SHORTLISTED FOR THE ONDAATJE PRIZE 2005

PEPSI AND MARIA Adam Zameenzad

'A beautifully
crafted, multi-
faceted book: a
highly dramatic and
gripping thriller and
a searing indictment
of cruelty and
inhumanity'—*New
Internationalist*
£8.99
ISBN 1 904559 06 9

Pepsi is a smart street kid in an unnamed South American country. His mother is dead and his father, a famous politician, has disowned him. He rescues the kidnapped Maria, but they must both escape the sadistic policeman Caddy whose obsession is to kill them – as personal vendetta and also as part of his crusade to rid the city of the 'filth' of street children. In this penetrating insight into the lives of the dispossessed, the author conveys the children's exhilarating zest for life and beauty, which triumphs over the appalling reality of their lives. Adam Zameenzad was born in Pakistan and lives in London. His previous novels have been published to great acclaim in many languages. This is his sixth novel.

UNCUT DIAMONDS
edited by Maggie Hamand

'The ability to pin down a moment or a mindset breathes from these stories … They're all stunning, full of wonderful characters'—
The Big Issue

£7.99
ISBN 1 904559 03 4

Vibrant, original stories showcasing the huge diversity of new writing talent in contemporary London. They include an incident in a women's prison; a spiritual experience in a motorway service station; a memory of growing up in sixties Britain and a lyrical West Indian love story. Unusual and sometimes challenging, this collection gives voice to previously unpublished writers from a wide diversity of backgrounds whose experiences – critical to an understanding of contemporary life in the UK – often remain hidden from view.

ANOTHER COUNTRY   Hélène du Coudray

'The descriptions of the refugee Russians are agonisingly lifelike' —review of 1st edition, *Times Literary Supplement*

£7.99
ISBN 1 904559 04 2

Ship's officer Charles Wilson arrives in Malta in the early 1920s, leaving his wife and children behind in London. He falls for a Russian émigrée governess, the beautiful Maria Ivanovna, and the passionate intensity of his feelings propels him into a course of action that promises to end in disaster. This prize-winning novel, first published in 1928, was written by an Oxford undergraduate, Hélène Héroys, who was born in Kiev in 1906. She went on to write a biography of Metternich, and three further novels.

THE THOUSAND-PETALLED DAISY
Norman Thomas

'This novel, both rhapsody and lament, is superb'—
Independent on Sunday

£7.99
ISBN 1 904559 05 0

Injured in a riot while travelling in India, 17-year-old Michael Flower is given shelter in a white house on an island. There, accompanied by his alter ego (his glove-puppet Mickey-Mack), he meets Om Prakash and his family, a tribe of holy monkeys, the beautiful Lila and a mysterious holy woman. Jealousy and violence, a death and a funeral, the delights of first love and the beauty of the landscape are woven into a narrative infused with a distinctive, offbeat humour. Norman Thomas was born in Wales in 1926. His first novel was published in 1963. He lives in Auroville, South India.

ON BECOMING A FAIRY GODMOTHER
Sara Maitland

'Funny, surreal tales
. . . magic and
mystery'—*Guardian*
'These tales
insistently fill the
vison'—*Times
Literary Supplement*
£7.99
ISBN 1 904559 00 X

Fifteen 'fairy stories' breathe new life into old legends and bring the magic of myth back into modern women's lives. What became of Helen of Troy, of Guinevere and Maid Marion? And what happens to today's mature woman when her children have fled the nest? Here is an encounter with a mermaid, an erotic adventure with a mysterious stranger, the story of a woman who learns to fly and another who transforms herself into a fairy godmother.

IN DENIAL Anne Redmon

'This is intelligent
writing worthy of
a large audience'—
The Times
'Intricate, thoughtful'
—*Times Literary
Supplement*
£7.99
ISBN 1 904559 01 8

In a London prison a serial offender, Gerry Hythe, is gloating over the death of his one-time prison visitor Harriet Washington. He thinks he is in prison once again because of her. Anne Redmon weaves evidence from the past and present of Gerry's life into a chilling mystery. A novel of great intelligence and subtlety, *In Denial* explores themes which are usually written about in black and white, but here are dealt with in all their true complexity.

LEAVING IMPRINTS Henrietta Seredy

'This mesmerising,
poignant novel
creates an intense
atmosphere'—
Publishing News
'Compelling ... full
of powerful events
and emotions'—
Oxford Times
£7.99
ISBN 1 904559 02 6

'At night when I can't sleep I imagine myself on the island.' But Jessica is alone in a flat by a park. She doesn't want to be there – she doesn't have anywhere else to go. As the story moves between present and past, gradually Jessica reveals the truth behind the compelling relationship that has dominated her life. 'With restrained lyricism, *Leaving Imprints* explores a destructive, passionate relationship between two damaged people. Its quiet intensity does indeed leave imprints. I shall not forget this novel'—Sue Gee, author of *The Hours of the Night*